Emilie's Song

by

Darlene Dauphin

authorHOUSE®

AuthorHouse™
1663 Liberty Drive
Bloomington, IN 47403
www.authorhouse.com
Phone: 1-800-839-8640

Published by AuthorHouse 01/18/2016

ISBN: 978-1-4389-0332-3 (sc)

Print information available on the last page.

This book is printed on acid-free paper.

Emilie's Song

1

The boy wore a tan tweed cap pulled tightly down over his mop of curly, black hair. He was cleanly clad and dressed in layers of quality winter clothing that included a lengthy, bright red scarf wound carefully about his neck. Unlike so many of the others around him, he wore clothing warm enough for this briskly chilling day. It was an unseasonably cold morning for New Orleans in November. People's faces reflected the bleakness of both the cold and of the Depression that held this city, as well as the country, firmly in its grip. The weather was an insult added to injury. Windy gusts swirled about the noisy street, swishing bits of debris here and there. The sharp, clip clop of the horses' hooves hitting the cobblestones created a rhythm in Antoine's ear. He dodged through the crowd, using that rhythm to keep him focused and intent upon his route. He turned the corner from St Claude onto Conti Street, knowing that the little house was just one block away. If he were lucky he would be able to see them as they sat down for breakfast. In front of the kitchen table, the pretty house had a big window surrounded by crisp white curtains that made it look like a framed picture. There he could see the man, woman and the small girl looking very much like a perfect portrait. Hiding tightly behind the gate, he was able to glimpse into the daily life of the little family. It had become a part of his routine to detour past this house at least three times a week as he made his way from Orleans Street. Someone, he decided, must keep an eye on her. After all, she still belonged to them. Antoine was alone in the early mornings because lately his brother, Bernard, went to the docks before school daily, earning coins by running errands for the men who labored there.

No one knew that Antoine came here to see his sister. He was extremely careful to be sure that even she didn't see him. There it was, the blue and white house that looked like a drawing from the pages of a storybook. A perfect white wooden fence bordered a small yard containing brightly hued flowers. The spots of color sprinkled heavily throughout the space always made him happy. Few houses here in this part of the city had such a front yard. Most often the steps led directly from the sidewalk to the front door. Other houses on the block looked to be connected one to the other. An orderly row of three wide steps led up to the pair of doors on every house down each block. The two doors were there because the buildings were divided into double residences for two families. As an exception, this house sat alone as a single family residence. Few other colored families lived on this section of the street. This he knew because he had spent time to examine the neighborhood carefully. It was important that he was clear on all the facts about where she lived. He needed to know that his sister was all right.

Emilie was three years old. She looked like those expensive chocolate colored dolls sold in the French Quarter shops. Her jet black hair was thick, long and straight enough that it had just the hint of a curl. Like all of their family, she had what was referred to as 'good' hair. Sometimes they sat in the garden while the lady combed Emilie's abundant hair. She lovingly styled and put ribbons in it. He thought that the lady probably had Emilie confused with a baby doll, usually changing her clothes several times a day. It was as though she thought that the girl was a toy, not a real little girl. Emilie looked to be patient enough about it. He never saw her pouting, or angry, nor upset. She happily did as the lady asked. But it worried him that she played by herself all of the time. Maybe she was lonely, but at least she seemed to be okay. He spent a short time peering through the fence, observing the morning routine inside the picturesque house. When the man stood up to leave, the boy turned his collar up higher and quickly ran away, not wanting the man to spot him. As long as they didn't know that he was watching them, Antoine hoped that everything was okay and Emilie would be safe there with the couple.

He had just a few minutes to get to school. Luckily the building was not very far away if he hurried. He wanted to stop going to school, but his mother had threatened him. Sally was a force to be reckoned with. She refused to allow it even though there were only a few more years of school readily available to the colored students. He could already read and write better than the average grownup that he knew. If he found some kind of job, maybe then Emilie could come home. He never quite understood why Sally had sent her away. Annie, he and his brother could have kept looking out for her. How much he missed his baby sister was all that he thought about sometimes. The three of them used to be together at home in the evenings with Annie most of the time since Sally was never around then anyway. People wondered why he called his mother by her name, but they were people who did not know her. He thought about how different their lives were than other folks, as he walked into the school just before the bell.

2

Some nosy people, who didn't know her, speculated that Sally was a 'sportin' woman because they observed her routine of spending so much time away from home. They only saw a pretty woman who spent her late afternoons and the majority of her evenings in the area of restaurants and speakeasies on the fringes of the French Quarter. This area contained places where some people felt unsafe and where many kept an eye over one shoulder. Sally was not someone who needed to do that. If necessary, she was capable of cold cocking a full-grown man. It had been necessary, once or twice. Standing six feet tall, Sally Langlois Tolliver was a stunningly beautiful woman. Her complexion was a perfect shade of pale saffron, framed by dense, lustrous locks of chestnut hair that lay in waves about her heart shaped face. Her gold flecked gray eyes and eye-catching figure turned many a head. A gentle dusting of freckles lay scattered from the bridge of her perfect nose to her sharply chiseled cheekbones. Her beauty, too, tended to bewilder people, especially men. When Sally had taken to wearing the new flapper style clothing, exposure of her long legs caused many a problem.

Her breathtaking figure was made for the body skimming dresses and short skirts.

Men sometimes did not understand that she dressed for her own pleasure, not theirs. Country boys sometimes got especially confounded. More than once some big overgrown kid from across the river spotted Sally and got excited, figuring that she was the answer to his prayers. Sally took no guff from any man, so these poor fellows always ended up somewhere slobbering dejectedly into a glass of beer. If Sally took the time to speak to them personally, it was even worse. Having experienced her loveliness up close, they truly felt a sense of loss. If the would be suitor tried to press his case with too much enthusiasm, an employee appeared at her side to discourage him. With her ownership of two thriving establishments, she had no shortage of assistance available to her.

The two boys, Antoine and Bernard, were the product of a short-lived early marriage. Sally laughingly told people that she had been a dumb country girl who married the first man who had made her heart skip a beat. Truthfully, she had married the man she loved from childhood. At eighteen her father finally allowed her to marry Bernard Langlois, who was already twenty and madly in love with Sally. He had big plans for his future and neither the cane fields, nor sharecropping, fit into them. Since decent work was hard to come by in that part of St John Parish, he kept talking about the war and how if he went in for an enlistment it might serve them. He decided that it was a chance for him to get some kind of job training, making it easy for them to move to New Orleans after the war was over. She had never wanted to agree, but when her period didn't come, she lessened her objections. Finally the birth of a beautiful son clarified the necessity for some imminent solution. St John Parish did not hold out any hope for the better life they wanted for the baby. They both knew that Bernard urgently needed to do something, but he continued making do with odd jobs for a year, or so. Finally, he enlisted, looking for the key to his young family's future. Sally was so proud of the way that her tall, handsome husband looked in his uniform and felt good showing him off whenever he returned on furlough.

Even her objections quieted for a moment. But as fate would have it, his unit shipped out to the war zone shortly after he was assigned to his first duty station. Then it seemed that he had barely arrived before he died there in France. Sally had not forgiven him for leaving them, let alone for dying.

At the funeral, everyone who saw the beautiful young widow with the two year old son felt badly. Sadder still, they saw her swollen belly and knew that she would give birth to another child very soon. Bernard had not been overseas six months before he perished in combat. His widow thought that it was the stupidest thing that she had ever heard. Bernard was not a coward, so she knew that it wasn't his fault in that way. But she had somehow known, and told him, that there were too many things that could go wrong. People saw that she was inconsolable and assumed that Sally's anger was grief.

Antoine had been born one month after his father died. The two boys were exactly alike except for their skin color. Bernard Jr. had been born almost nine months to the day after their marriage. Her mother in law had been heard to make a catty remark about the child's skin color and light eyes. The baby was indeed fair-skinned like Sally and his eyes were blue when he was born, though later they would seem more of a green color. Sally's Aunt Jess had heard her whisper loudly to one of her friends at a church social.

"I don't know who that yella' gal thinks she's foolin'. Bernard can't get no blue-eyed babies. We ain't never had no blue eyed babies in this family. I got my questions."

Sally had cried and cried. When Bernard discovered what had upset her, he had angrily gone and confronted his mother. Since he had no question about the child's paternity, he assured her that he would not accept shabby treatment of his wife. Despite his mother's protests, Bernard moved with his young family to the next settlement so that Sally could be nearer her parents.

Most people saw that the baby looked exactly like his father even though he had his mother's pale skin. Bernard was a tall man with skin as smooth and luscious as the frosting on a chocolate cake, with color was so even that it appeared to have been mixed to perfect proportions and spread from a bowl. Laughingly, the young friends of the couple called them 'Chocolate and Vanilla'.

When the baby kept his paleness, Bernard's mother had more to say. Sally's own mother had finally found it necessary to confront the woman at the next church event. She realized that the woman's problem stemmed from her own personal issues about color. Everyone knew that it was the constant wild card in the lives of colored people. Due to the heritage of slavery, it was virtually impossible to predict a child's skin color even when both parents were of similar shades. Sally never knew exactly what her mother said to the woman, but she never again made comment about her son's family.

When Antoine was born, he looked exactly like both his father and brother. The two boys were identical except that the new baby had his father's complexion. His eyes, however, were of an even paler shade of gray than his mother's and his hair somewhat straighter than that of his brother.

The newly widowed Sally had hung around the parish for a couple of years doing the only work available, cleaning houses, cooking and taking in laundry. Since she was not afraid of hard work and the pay was better, she had even gone to the cane fields momentarily. Strong enough to swing the scythe effectively, she persevered until the men finally ran her away. None of them seemed to understand that she simply did not want to be bothered. Her physical strength had come in handy more than once walking down the country lanes.

Her anger at Bernard had subsided, just barely. How dare he leave her after all those years of promises? She had known that she would marry him from the time that she was eight years old with two thick red plaits hanging down her back. One day she had looked at him and it was different. Her best friend thought that she was crazy until they were about fourteen. Bernard had always seemed to give her a special smile and by the time she was sixteen, even he knew that he didn't have a chance. The willowy girl was all that he could see. His friends teased him unceasingly because by then it was clear to everyone. Bernard was the only man at whom she had ever looked. After he died and she was still stuck in St John Parish, no one seemed to understand that. One tall, lanky fellow named Red Charbonnet had told her that it was a waste for her not to have a man around when she was "just ripe", while willingly volunteering his services to her in her 'time of need'. She had taken Bernard's shotgun and run his rusty red nappy-haired behind back down the lane. It had been almost funny to see the shocked expression on his face. Several others like him had required similar convincing. But when the white men started the same behavior, she knew that she had to go. It was as though her female scent was on the wind and the hound dogs of both colors were chasing her to ground. So off she went to New Orleans.

Her parents joyfully cared for the boys for over a year in the kind of arrangement common to many country families. She worked hard, sent enough money home so that her boys wouldn't be a financial burden to her folks. The rest went into a savings book. Unbeknownst to her, her parents also saved every penny of the money that she sent home to them. They called it Sally's Rainy Day Fund. Thrift was a family habit.

On the early summer evening that she walked out of the back entrance of the hotel where she worked and saw her father standing there, Sally was certain that something must be very wrong. It was. Her mother had died the night before. Her father looked as though he had aged ten years in the few months since December. She had managed to spend more than a week over there when she took the toys and clothes for Christmas. It had been hard to arrange, but she had worked four weeks straight and traded days off with two different people. The effort had been worth it purely for the pleasure of seeing the looks on her sons' faces. The boys were growing more rapidly than she could keep track. Her mother had seemed tired and wan even then, however she assured Sally that it was only some kind of a bug. Her daddy now said that the doctors had told him it had been something wrong with her blood. Momma had known about her medical condition for a while, but chose to tell no one. Having the boys around helped her to hang onto her life as long as possible. Sally was her only child and Momma determined that helping this child to get her life on track was her most important task as a mother. Both of her parents felt that life had given Sally a bad hand, losing Bernard the way that she had.

Momma loved her precious grandsons and regretted that she would not live to see them grow up. By caring for them, she told her husband, at least she had the blessing of getting to know them well. Though they were rough and tumble little boys, sharing hugs and kisses with her was among their favorite activities. Had fate been kinder, Sally's parents mused, they might have had sons also, because neither of them had intended for her to be an only child. Watching the boys grow had salved some of that acute disappointment. It was a mutual admiration society. The boys would miss their "MeMa".

Sally was able to go home to St John Parish and stay for three weeks when her mother died. Her coworkers made this possible by filling shifts for her as she had often done for many of them. Since she chose to have no personal life, she had been happy to cover for anyone needing time off, often at a minute's notice. The extra work served to fill up the huge void that was her personal life. Because Sally's life was focused only on work, she had helped others who now offered a hand in her time of need.

One of the women at the hotel arranged the connection with a lady from her church who would care for the two little boys when she returned to New Orleans. Tucked safely away in her purse was the Rainy Day Fund that her father now passed along to her. Valerie Broussard was a widow without any family who welcomed the daily companionship. It was the perfect arrangement for a long time as Mrs. Broussard became like another grandmother to Bernard and Antoine, while only charging a minimal fee for the services. Sally moved from the sparse room that she rented on Miro Street to a little house nearer Orleans Street, where the older woman lived. On pleasant mornings she dropped them off, but Mrs. Broussard insisted on coming to Sally's place on winter days when she felt the weather was too cold. Pneumonia had claimed the life of her only son at three and another child never came to bless her life, so she was extra careful about any chills and drafts. Just as she retired from working, her 'Mr. Broussard' had died and 'Miss Valerie' felt her future to be bleak and empty. The lovely young woman and the two adorable boys became the beloved family that she never had. Sally and her family seemed to be a godsend for Valerie. Day in and day out, the two women intermingled their lives. Holidays meant shared meals and exchanged gifts. The daily schedule often included long talks over a simple, but tasty, supper. Both women needed the additional dimension in their lives.

When the boys were six and almost eight, Mrs. Broussard died suddenly leaving Sally totally bereft. Not only had Valerie seemed completely healthy, but their lives had reached a perfect comfort level in the past few years. Sally had work, Mrs. Broussard and the boys, just enough to fill her heart. She didn't date or go out looking for another man to complete her life despite the older woman's encouragement. This had been enough, but now she must adjust. Weighing heavily on her mind also was the fact that the boys had once again lost their primary caregiver. How their lives would now change, became her concern.

3

Mrs. Broussard's wake was on a Friday night. The funeral, or Dismissal, was on a Saturday morning at a flower filled church on St Peter Street where a procession of people said wonderful things about Miss Valerie. Sally sat quietly in a stunned state. The sensation was that she was sleepwalking through the whole thing. Loss of this second mother figure in so few years was even harder than she could have imagined.

On the following Tuesday evening when Sally rounded the corner toward home, a man stood on her front steps. She didn't know him, but he looked fairly harmless. A well-dressed older colored man, he carried a weathered brown leather satchel of some kind. Her thought was that he looked like a salesman. Sure enough, when she reached the porch she could see the navy blue and white National Life Insurance insignia attached to his briefcase. For some reason both boys promptly greeted the man with familiarity. They seemed to know him.

"Hello, boys. Good evening, Mrs. Langlois", he put his hand out. "I am Edward Dupree from National Life."

The man was so very proper in his speech and manners. Sally admired his 'away' sounding speech. But she thought it funny that anyone believed she possessed a single copper to invest in anything. Even the new babysitter was going to cost so much more. She was trying so hard to continue to be thrifty. To be sure, because her mother taught her to be courteous, she shook his hand anyway.

"Nice to meet you, Mr. Dupree." She paused at the top step.

The weather was pleasant enough this evening and the boys could play outside for a couple of hours. She settled herself on the step. The boys quickly took the cue as an okay to play on the sidewalk.

"Ma'am, I came by to speak to you about an important business matter. You were acquainted with Mrs. Valerie Broussard?" He rapidly followed with, "It is an official question that I have to ask."

The man sat down and started to open his briefcase.

"Yes sir. Mrs. Broussard was real close to my boys and me. She was like family since they came down here… started off babysitting, but we ended up loving her." A single enormous tear dragged its way down her face slowly.

"Mrs. Langlois, she evidently thought the same of you.

About two years ago she made you her primary heir. This means that you are the beneficiary of her life insurance policies, as well as of all her worldly goods. I am the National agent and as her friend, I was also witness to her last will and testament."

Sally found it hard to make sense of what the man said. The last few days had been difficult, more because of the absence of her friend than of anything else.

"But didn't she have a niece, or something, in Chicago I thought?"

"Yes ma'am, she did. But since she had no real relationship with that woman, I mean she didn't even know her. But she surely loved you and your boys..." His voice trailed off.

Sally started to cry in earnest. She had not allowed herself to grieve up to now. There had been so many things to do... getting ready for the funeral... finding another babysitter... adjusting her schedule to accommodate the different location. Dupree observed the genuine sadness gripping the young woman.

"Ma'am, I am sorry for your loss. Mrs. Broussard was a fine woman. I was acquainted with both her and her husband for many years. I do know that your family gave her that something that she never expected to have, something that she had given up on. She dearly loved you and your boys."

Sally looked at the man carefully, now realizing that he was familiar to her. It was her habit to not pay too much personal attention to the men she met in the course of day to day life, especially outside of work. This way she avoided a lot of trouble. But now she remembered seeing him from time to time when she picked up the boys.

"Yes sir, we loved her too. Mrs. Broussard was special to us. I don't know what I would have done without her. But how can she just give us something when we are not blood kin?"

"Mrs. Langlois, a person has the right to make a bequest to whomever they please. She loved you like family. There is also the matter of the house on Orleans Street and a flat up near Claiborne."

Sally was beginning to be really mystified. Was this man truly saying that Miss Valerie had left her the house she had lived in and another one as well?

"Mr. Dupree, was it? Sir, are you saying that she left me all those things? Left them to me?"

The look on her face was incredulous, causing the large gray eyes to be as round as circles. Such things just didn't happen to her. Except for the love of her parents, her adult life had been filled with bad fortune. Sally even viewed her fabulous looks as questionable luck and they continued to primarily be a source of pain. Bernard was the only man who ever took her seriously. Other men thought that she looked like comfort material for their beds. Women were often jealous. Having heard the phrase "uppity high yellow bitch" muttered under some insecure woman's breath too often, she carried herself as plainly as possible to avoid trouble.

"Yes, that is exactly what I am telling you. We can go to the lawyer's office tomorrow and you can sign the papers and it will all be yours officially."

"This a lot to sink in, Mr. Dupree. I can't go tomorrow. I have to work…"

"Mrs. Langlois, you do get a lunch period, don't you? Mr. Fouchet's office is in the suite of offices just next door to the hotel, right there on Canal Street. He's a nice white fellow, a Frenchman and he will get it handled quickly. He already knows all about you."

After agreeing to meet the men the next day, Sally called the boys to her and took them inside. The small dwelling was what was called a 'shotgun' house. It consisted of three real rooms, one in front of the other with a bathroom and porch off the kitchen, which was at the rear. At least this one had the advantage of paint that was fresh and pretty. And it was clean. Sally took good care of the boys and was what the old folks called a 'house proud' woman. Looking around her, she realized that if today's events were real, she would now have the tidy house on Orleans Street to call her own.

It was bigger than the one in which she now lived, with three other rooms in addition to the kitchen, bath, living and dining rooms. There was also a nice gallery, or porch, for her to relax and the boys to play. Originally, the couple hoped for a large family. Mrs. Broussard's husband worked hard as a stevedore on the docks all his life. Miss Valerie spent her working life in housekeeping at a hotel for thirty-five years. Frugality was the watchword in the Broussard home. Miss Valerie mentioned to Sally once that the house was paid for. It was just something that Sally remembered, thinking that it was nice that the older woman's life was comfortably cushioned. At the same time she wondered if she might ever possess a cushion of any sort. Her adult life so far showed no positive signs. Since Bernard died, her only options kept her constantly working like a dog and she could see no relief in sight. Guiltily, she realized that her friend's death would now give her some measure of relief.

On the next day, Sally said nothing of her good fortune to anyone at work. When lunchtime rolled around, she hurried next door. Still, she held some subconscious doubt that the two men would be there. On the way to work, she had stopped and surreptitiously looked up the lawyer's name in the directory for the office building next door. An *Andre Fouchet, Esq.* was indeed listed in suite 308. She smoothed her simple black broadcloth skirt and white blouse. Glancing in the mirrored surface of the door, she saw that her appearance was satisfactory. As she walked up the flights of stairs, she said a quick prayer that there was no catch to any of this.

"There you are Mrs. Langlois." Edward Dupree stood and greeted her as she entered. The waiting room was nicely appointed, but small. No one else was present at the moment. There was a small windowed enclosure upon which Dupree softly rapped twice. As promptly as he did, a fastidiously dressed dark haired white man emerged from a side door. Shaking her hand, he introduced himself to her and welcomed her into his office. Sally had never seen an office like this. It was filled with row upon row of beautiful leather bound books. She recalled that the Bible at her parent's home looked this same way. None of the few other books in her experience were as rich looking. Around the room, plants were placed in the same manner as those in the fancy suites at the hotel. Each item of furniture was constructed of gleaming wood and sumptuous upholstery in richly muted colors. For some reason, Sally instantly trusted these two men. Fouchet treated her like any lady, not just a dumb country girl from across the river. He pulled out her chair, offered her refreshment and proceeded to carefully explain the bequest to her after a brief conversation.

Valerie Broussard had been a woman of some means. Sally knew that she babysat for companionship more than anything, but it turned out that she had saved all of that money. According to the weekly entries in her passbook, she deposited every penny that Sally had paid her. She left Sally the sum of almost ten thousand dollars in three life insurance policies, over thirty thousand dollars in cash and the two houses with all of her worldly goods. An inherited piece of valuable jewelry was bequeathed to the niece up in Illinois. Sally sat numb and dumbfounded. That anyone would have given such an amazing gift to her, plain country Sally, was beyond belief. Even though she had been told, it was still new and strange. When she signed her name, the young woman was in shock. In a fog she moved through the afternoon tasks at work. As she checked out for the day, it occurred to her that she didn't really have to go back to work at the hotel. She was a woman of some means now! Work was something that she chose to do, but she opted to think through her choices carefully. She would make a real plan before she did anything different at all. One thing was certain, she and her sons could move into their new home. It was just the first week of the month, so she would have plenty of time to move into the Orleans Street house. She would go by tomorrow and tell her landlord.

The Binetti family ran the little store at the corner. It was 1925 and everything still boomed along in the post war mode. Stocks were flying at an astronomical rate. Money was plentiful for most. A whole block of houses on that side of the street belonged to the Binettis, who were benevolent landlords because they lived in the neighborhood. The big house faced the side street and the store was built into the first floor basement. Rumor had it that Victor Binetti sold wine that he brewed in a huge vat located in that same area. Binetti's father was often seen wearing a heavy purple-stained apron as he moved about the house and store, validating the whispers. Prohibition had created many such home-based businesses. One such entrepreneur in the neighborhood used fruit from his backyard tree to brew peach brandy in his bathtub. A woman in the next block brewed a popular plum wine, said to be as tasty as Mogen David. It was the poorest kept secret in the area. Sally believed in minding her own business and did not care about any of them. Her only concern about her landlord was that he should treat her fairly without any undue personal attention. Binetti was a family man who caused her no problems. As such, she was accorded the courtesies given all good tenants.

On the next morning Sally stopped by the store before she started out for work. Mrs. Binetti's eyebrows rose, but she understood when Sally told her about moving to the Broussard house. Most interesting to Sally was the woman's quick questions about the flat on Claiborne Street. Evidently she knew that Valerie had owned it also. Sight unseen, she said, she was willing to purchase the building. Perhaps her landlady had always had her eye on the place, or had she just developed an interest since Miss Valerie died? Sally told her that she would advise the lawyer who was handling it. Without acknowledging her ownership, she had gently deflected her offer.

For the rest of the week, Sally considered the ramifications of her inheritance. Her future, and that of her sons, could be changed forever if she made the appropriate choices. Sally vowed to make wise decisions and sat down first to make a list of their immediate needs and the options to fill those needs. By that weekend, she had bought a small wagon and horse to get her around. In the next block, there was still a livery stable that serviced the surrounding area. On Friday afternoon, she bundled up the boys and took the trip to St John Parish. She was no stranger to travel by buggy, but it had been a while since she had handled a rig. An exhausted Sally pulled from the country lane up into her father's yard. After peeking out of the curtains with uncertainty, he came happily rushing out to greet them. After unloading first the two sleepy boys, and then the assorted bags, they sat down around the kitchen table. His face was wreathed in smiles, but he could barely contain his curiosity.

"Baby girl, it's so good to see the three of you! You should have let me know that you were coming! I could have had a pot of something good simmering on the stove."

Sally glanced over at the large black iron stove in the corner of the kitchen. It served dual purposes in winter, heating and cooking. Despite his disclaimer, an aromatic pot sat simmering.

"Papa, I know there's some red beans and rice over there. You don't want to share today?" She laughed.

In the kerosene lamplight, a gentle look of concern could be seen crossing his face. His deep voice was warm and loving.

"Honey, you know what I mean. I could have fixed something special. But, I wasn't expecting you all. After Miss Valerie's funeral, I could have brought those boys back with me if I had known you were planning to come up. Is everything all right? Whose rig is that outside?" He repeated himself, "Is something wrong?"

"Papa, everything is fine. In fact, it's better than fine. That's why I came all the way up here. I wanted to talk to you. And the rig is mine."

She was so touched by her father's continued concern for her. So many parents seemed to push their children from the nest, then put them out of mind. There were families nearby that seldom saw or heard from their adult children. Maybe it was different between them because she was an only child. Large families, maybe, needed to worry more about their children being able to take care of themselves. Whatever the reason, Sally was genuinely glad that her father continued to demonstrate that he loved her still. Reaching across the table, she touched his hand affectionately.

"You know, sometimes good things can come out of the darkest times, Papa. I can't believe this, but Miss Valerie left me an inheritance, a sizeable inheritance. The insurance man came over on Tuesday evening and told me. Then I went to the lawyer's office and he gave me all the information."

Rene Arceneaux looked at his daughter with a solemn expression. He took a deep sip from his mug of coffee, staring into its depths. The interior of the aged ceramic cup was discolored by the years being filled with chicory-laced coffee, but the stains were familiar and comforting.

Sally's beauty had always been a source of concern for him. Around every corner, he could see the possible pitfalls and traps awaiting her. The world was sometimes such an evil place. It was his familiar role to worry for her.

"Who are these people, Sally? What do they expect you to do for this money? Is it money? How much money are we talking about?" The questioning was gentle, but persistent.

"Can you trust this lawyer? So many of them are shysters, child."

Sally held up her hand between them. "Papa, stop. I understand your concerns. But, I saw it all in black and white. I'll show you the papers. Papa, you know that I am very careful. There's no catches to any of this. Miss Valerie left me her house, another flat near Claiborne and some money in policies and cash. She had a niece in up Chicago, but she left her just some family jewelry. Papa, she loved us, just like we loved her."

"Baby, I'm sorry and I know that you are a smart, grown woman now. It's just so rare that anything like that happens, especially to Colored. It's like some kind of storybook thing. Lord almighty! You deserve to have something good happen to you." He shook his head in apologetic disbelief.

"Papa, I know. I read it carefully. It's all true. The lawyer is a man named Andre' Fouchet. He treated me real nice, Papa. The National Life man was a real friend of Miss Valerie and that lawyer had represented her for years."

The enormity of his daughter's stroke of good fortune began to dawn upon Rene. He'd still need to see it to believe it, but so far it sounded like a real blessing.

When Sally pulled out her copies to show him, he finally accepted that he was not dreaming.

"What do you plan to do now? If you are careful that nest egg could serve you for the rest of your life."

"That's what I came to talk about. Papa, I been thinking all week and I came to some conclusions. This is an opportunity, Papa, an opportunity to get further ahead than just 'getting by'. Don't forget, I am young, healthy and not afraid of hard work. In the last few years I have learned most everything about the running of the hotel restaurant where I work. Papa, I been there for over four years. And I'm the person that Mr. Robert depends on. I'm the one that everybody comes to. Whenever Mr. Robert is out, he tells people to come to me. Maybe the Maitre De looks like he's the one, but I'm the one doing the work. Papa, I think that I want to run my own restaurant. The flat could be used for that. Really, Papa! Anything that I don't know, I can sure learn."

Stopping only to tuck the boys into bed, the pair sat and talked for most of the night. Rene was as excited for his daughter, as she was for herself. He pledged to assist her in every way possible. Sally finally left him sitting at the table. Since his wife's death, he didn't like to go to bed as early. This was the time that the sharp edge of his loneliness became so acute. Most difficult for him was the absence of their intimate rituals. At times he used to help her with the hundred nightly strokes faithfully given to her heavy, thick hair. Before she died, she had become weak and depended upon him for so much. None of these extra tasks ever felt like a chore. Now he suffered their loss. As the fire burned itself down to embers, he opened the door on the front of the stove and smothered the last of the red hot coals. His eyes were good and heavy by the time that he retired to the darkened quiet of his room.

Before his eyes closed, a special prayer of thanks crossed his lips that night.

Curling up in the room that she grew up in, Sally reviewed this past week in her life. Now that she had shared her plan with her father, it was even more crystal clear to her. Sally was satisfied that she was capable of being successful. Her education was adequate since she had finished the highest grade in the colored school in St John Parish. Learning had always come easy for her. Besides what she learned in school, she used to read the magazines and books from the ladies' houses when she did day work. Sally felt secure about her level of understanding. One thing was certain, she knew how the restaurant worked, every part of it. Most importantly, Sally was convinced that she would do it because she wanted this more than anything. As she fell asleep that evening, the complete plan had hatched in her brain.

The next morning Rene had one question for his daughter. "Why", he asked her, "Did you buy that rig outside?"

Sally didn't understand his question.

"What do you mean? Papa, it's a good horse, not old. The rig is lightweight enough to serve me in the city. It was a good bargain."

"Sally, this is 1925. A young person like you should have a more modern attitude. You are going to be running your own business and all."

It was very early, she thought and the woman could not, for the life of her, understand what her father meant. She looked at him quizzically. Her father laughed and beckoned for her to follow him outside. The now wide awake boys ran about in circles, happy to be free in the sweet air of the country morning. Rene led her to the large structure that had served as a barn when Rene's father had owned the property. Inside, he proudly showed her the Ford Model T that he had purchased just the day before. He explained to his daughter that his trip into the city to the funeral had convinced him to step into the automobile age. Livery stables were getting more and more scarce, as well as more expensive. On the way out of the city, a dealership for motorcars caught his eye and he made an immediate decision.

The small group loaded into the car for a ride. Sally was even more excited than the boys, feeling a sense of freedom almost intoxicating to her. Just riding was not enough. Before the weekend was over, not only could she drive the machine as well as Rene himself, she had made the choice to step into this new age as well. After all she had the funds to do so.

Bright and early on Monday morning, Sally made the return trip into New Orleans with Rene Arceneaux and the boys following his daughter's rig to a dealer's location. After a spirited bit of negotiation, a delighted Sally drove away in her own vehicle. A trip to the livery took care of the horse and rig. She rid herself of it as easily as she had obtained it.

Sally made no other quick changes to her life. She continued to work at the hotel for another year while she made conscious effort to verify her knowledge of the small things of which she was unsure. Instead of driving her new automobile downtown, she continued to catch the public streetcar. It was not her desire to titillate anyone's interest at work, or to appear above her station. The automobile was part of her new life, which was still in process. A secret joy filled her when she thought of the gleaming tan sedan. Meanwhile the flat was being remodeled. Before, the building had been a beautifully constructed Victorian duplex. A second floor was remodeled to include three private dining rooms, as well as an office with an adjoining dressing room. The remainder of the space upstairs was left vacant. Her papa, who had built things all his life, was supervising the crew of carpenters and craftsmen. His temporary move into town to help her had been a godsend. It gave him something to do and the boys enjoyed being with their 'Papaw' in the evenings. Only the lawyer and her father knew of her plans. Once he met the lawyer, Rene agreed with his daughter's assessment of him. Fouchet handled all of the permits and general red tape. All papers were promptly and correctly filed in her name. He was as aboveboard as he had been with the affairs of the will and inheritance. Zoning at the location was appropriate for business as well as residences. Not a single hitch appeared in obtaining the necessary papers. Sally Langlois was on her way to being her own boss lady before her twenty-seventh birthday. Even she knew that this was no mean feat in New Orleans in 1925, especially for a colored girl from the country.

4

Most of the year, New Orleans weather is hot and humid. When the thermometer rises, it feels like steam comes up out of the swamplands to engulf the city's streets. The muggy air becomes a living thing. People are able to touch and feel its presence. When the winter decides to make itself a viable entity, the city goes into shock. The looks on the faces of people in the streets tell the story. Startled glances passed from one to the other as if to verify that the temperature is, indeed, as low as it feels to you. On this chilly day, people exchange such glances.

The boy, Antoine, rubs his hands together to rid them of the prickly chill. The small school classroom is heated by a stove, but has not had an opportunity to completely warm up yet. Unlike some of the other children, he has good winter clothing. He feels badly for the boy who sits across from him whose tattered clothing is virtually threadbare. It is easy to see that he has stuffed newspapers inside his jacket and pants for an added layer of insulation. Many of the students did not bother to come to school today. Cold weather is the avowed enemy of the poor.

This is especially true in the Deep South where this forbidding weather is rare and too many of the Colored are poor.

In this neighborhood, many of the children do not have the sturdy shoes so necessary on a day like this. Antoine feels lucky in so many ways since he and his brother have not just good clothing, shoes, enough food and a decent place to live, but their mother even owned an automobile, which really set them apart. Sally has always given them all that they need. He knows that she is a good mother despite her long hours away from home. For this reason, he fails to understand why she sent Emilie away. Maybe it was because of money, since they do live better than most colored families and some of the white families nearby.

Late at night when she is alone, he has seen Sally look at the small picture of Emilie and cry. He believes that she loves the baby girl in her heart of hearts, but he thinks that Sally is a hard woman. When she first sent Emilie away, the boys assumed that it was just for a visit. The nice couple, who came to the house to get her, were not strangers. Several times before, he remembered that they had been guests for dinner. The woman was some kind of cousin to his mother, he recalled. At the time both she and her husband seemed to be taken with Emilie. The woman acted especially strange. She seemed almost to fall into a swoon, much like a child who had eaten too many sweets. He saw the woman touch Emilie's hair over and over. She kept leaning forward to stare at the tiny perfect face and smile. Her own face must have hurt from all of the smiling that she did.

Emilie was like a miniature queen who allowed herself to be worshipped by ordinary people. The woman jumped to feed her and to cut things for her. Antoine asked to be excused from the room because the woman made him sick. Emilie was a pretty little girl, he knew that, but this woman fawned over her like a lovesick puppy.

It occurred to him that Bernard had never yet reacted to her leaving. Antoine thought that his brother must care, but not once did he say anything about it. When Antoine tried to make him talk about her he refused, saying that it wouldn't do any good. Sally had only said that Emilie was going to go home with the people. She never said why, just as she never once discussed Michael's absence, even though he had become the only father they had ever known. Both boys hurt about Michael, but they were afraid to even mention his name. Likewise, they had no idea what happened to him. He was simply no longer there.

Emilie was another story. It had taken Antoine three months to find the people who had her. He remembered that the man's wagon had a business name painted on the side, *Rolande Drayage*. He hung out near the supply depot for many afternoons until he saw the man again. Luckily, the man didn't notice him, so Antoine followed him from there. On that day, he spotted Emilie sitting quietly in the flower filled yard, he stood there and started to cry. He supposed that it was because he spent the most time with her. After she sent Annie away, for a short time Sally used to take them all to the home of that lady with one blue eye. He always felt that he needed to look out for the baby. Though the woman who watched them was kind enough, she seemed to equate picking Emilie up in her arms with spoiling her. She baked cookies for them and spoke nicely to them, but Antoine did not appreciate her treatment of the baby. It felt as though she ignored her. Antoine was the youngest and he felt that babies needed to be held onto sometimes. Whenever he said anything to Bernard, his brother teased him. He asked Antoine if he wanted a doll baby. The younger boy didn't like dolls, but he loved his baby sister.

On the day that he found her she was dressed in a snowy white dress, a pinafore dress. All the layers of fabric were starched and the color was almost blindingly white in the brilliant spring sunshine. The lady put ribbons in Emilie's glossy black hair, something that Sally never did. Somehow Sally always seemed a bit strange about Emilie. One day the boys just arrived home and found Sally in bed surrounded by pillows, with a baby next to her. No one even warned them ahead of time. She hadn't gotten all fat and puffy, like most other women did. That was when Michael still lived with them. Both boys liked Michael from the first time that Sally introduced him. No one could have been happier than they were when Sally married him. To be truthful, they loved him. Because they had never known their own father, they appreciated having a man around.

Sally was different when Michael was there. She acted kind of soft and she smiled a lot, too. The lady where Emilie lived was soft. She smiled all the time and waited on Emilie hand and foot. Antoine thought that the little girl might be playing some kind of game. She knew that the lady wanted her to be happy and maybe she even knew that she made the lady happy. When he watched, he saw that Emilie acted as though she was perfectly content letting the woman run around behind her. He kept coming back to watch anyway, because Emilie belonged to them.

What Antoine didn't know was that the small girl knew that he watched her. One thing that he was correct about was that she absolutely reveled in the attention that Mommy Cora gave her. Her real mommy had not been like Mommy Cora. She was pretty to look at, but she no longer paid attention to Emilie like Mommy Cora did. Since her daddy went away, sometimes it seemed that she didn't even like looking at Emilie anymore. So, Emilie was perfectly happy right here for now.

Knowing that her brother came to see that she was okay did make the little girl feel happier. That first day that he saw her, she was having a tea party in the yard in her own miniature gazebo. Daddy Albert built a gazebo for her that contained its own matching table and chairs, just her size. She spent long afternoons having tea parties and conducting classes for her dolls. Mommy Cora also fashioned special dolls for her. Before she had Emilie to care for, making rag dolls for the shops in the French Quarter was what she enjoyed most. This talent was used to amuse Emilie to no end. She sat patiently beside Cora and watched her create the exquisitely detailed pretend girls. Emilie's favorite doll was one that Mommy Cora magically constructed to look just like her. Emilie decided that she was the luckiest little girl in the world.

After the nuns dismissed them from classes, Antoine located his brother. Because it was so cold today, Bernard figured that he might earn a handful of coins running to pick up the hot containers of coffee with chicory for the men this afternoon. He had enlisted Antoine's assistance for the weather affected increase in orders. Bernard already exhibited a promise of the same business savvy that his mother had. For a short while Sally had allowed her oldest son to help her at the café in the afternoon, whetting his entrepreneurial interest. But after Michael was gone, he was left to his own devices. Sally didn't know about the children's business enterprise. If she had known that her sons were hanging about the rough and tumble world of stevedores, dockworkers and longshoremen, the boys would be forced into someone's care again. It hadn't been easy to convince her that they were now old enough to look out for themselves in the afternoons. Any worry that she might have had would have been unwarranted, since several of the workers were men from the neighborhood around Orleans Street. These men admired the enterprising spirit of the brothers and kept an eye out for them as well. 'Miz Sally's boys' were safe because they were who they were.

After Michael and the baby were both gone, Sally became numb to almost everything around her personal life. Her sons took advantage of that time. They were, however, careful to not encourage the interest of any of the ladies in the neighborhood. Sally would have pulled out the razor strap if anyone told her that the boys were seen doing anything that some adult did not approve of. Even nosy Mrs. Boudreaux, the old lady with the big butt, hadn't ever noticed anything out of sorts with Sally's boys. And she was always asking them if they were okay, or if they needed anything. Like the men working on the docks, the neighborhood women kept an eye open also. But, the boys understood the rules. They were always careful to come home together. No one ever saw them argue or fight with each other. As far as the outside world knew, Bernard and Antoine were perfect little gentlemen. They had long ago learned to be a team.

Today the two boys ran the errands quickly together, earning the money that they had counted on. Certainly no one had told either of the boys that Sally needed money. They heard other people talk about needing money all the time. Things could have changed since Michael's disappearance. It had to be the reason that she gave Emilie away. Why else would someone give away a child?

Today the boys had earned almost four dollars before and after school. Immediately after the bell, the pair quickly hustled their way to the docks where some of the workers gave them as much as a dime to pick up coffee. It was especially chilly along the busy waterfront and the delivery of the steamy cups of coffee was appreciated.

The plan was to raise one hundred dollars and give it to Sally as a gift. So far they had earned seventeen dollars and thirty-one cents. That was a fortune to some in today's economy. If their mother had that money maybe Emilie could come home. Or so Antoine thought.

As the boys grew up, Sally had little idea as to what they were thinking. Sally knew that she should be closer to them, but they did have each other. They had always been together. She was the one left alone. The two of them were close to twins physically. There was only two inches or so difference in their heights. She was certain that it would vanish as they reached adulthood. Both were probably going to end up tall like Bernard, but then her father was tall too.

At first, before Michael, her problem was that seeing them was harder each day because they were two miniature versions of their father. The both of them were exactly like Bernard. It often seemed that they grew by the day. Always, they became more and more like him, just contrasting versions of the beautiful man that she had loved and married. It was so disconcerting to look at them. Most of all it was heartbreaking that they had no father. Bernard Jr. had those arresting blue-green eyes and sandy hair. Antoine's skin was even smoother, richer chocolate than his father's had been, as though rich dollops of mocha were stirred into the mix. His eyes were of such a pale gray shade that they were lighter than those of the older boy. But one thing remained consistent, the features of the two of them were identical, identically Bernard's. Sally could hardly bear to look at them because of the acute pain that she still felt. Bernard would have been a proud father to such smart and handsome sons. Michael certainly seemed to love them like they were his own.

The boys' lives were exceedingly comfortable. Even though they were unaware of it, a lady came to clean and do laundry while they were at school. These days Sally needed the time for precious sleep. Her working hours grew longer and longer. She usually left shortly before the boys came home from school. Also without their knowledge, someone kept an eye on them every day. Sally gave a few dollars every week to Mrs. Boudreaux next door, who faithfully gave a comprehensive report on their behavior. Antoine was a bit more of a dreamer than his big brother, but they were both very smart, well behaved boys. Progress Reports from the nuns were never less than glowing for both of them.

5

Sally failed to consider the degree of love and attachment that her boys possessed for the little girl she had placed in the care of Cora and Albert Rolande. Cora was her second cousin who had come over from the country a few years before Sally had. Her marriage to Albert came after a brief, intense courtship. Cora was a lovely woman of simple needs. She had a good man who loved her. Her home was immaculately kept. A needle and thread were instruments of great artistry in her hands. Cora made clothes for people, more for the joy of doing it than for the money. People said that her rag dolls sold for a lot of money in the fancy shops catering to tourists in the Quarter. Sally's contact with Cora came when someone offered her name as that of an extremely skilled seamstress. Upon coming to the neat little house, Sally was delighted to find her cousin Cora, a sweet, good person who had an almost interminable amount of energy. She had been so very happy to see Sally.

There was eight years difference in their ages, so Sally had not yet married when Cora embarked across the river to live. The far reaches of St John Parish had eventually not had anything to offer Cora either. At twenty-five she ventured to the city, already a definite spinster by country standards. Despite her pretty features, flawless cinnamon complexion, glorious head of hair and exquisitely petite figure, she remained unmarried and unclaimed. Albert had been the son of her landlady. Old Mrs. Rolande was beside herself with happiness when the romance had begun to blossom. Her son was always so particular about womenfolk.

Her dream was to see him married with a houseful of children, but Albert had not cooperated. He was a good Christian man who worked very hard building up his hauling business. His ambition just didn't seem to leave enough time for him to meet the right woman. Several times there were women at church who looked like good prospects, but Albert never warmed to any of them. Most notably among these young ladies, for Marie, was the pretty island girl named Camille. Thrilled to no end by her lovely singsong voice, Mrs. Rolande was additionally taken with her industrious nature. Despite her work schedule cleaning at one of the larger hotels, it seemed that she popped by the house with loaves of her delicious home-baked bread at least twice a week. Marie despaired that Albert just did not respond to her. Clearly she was making herself available to him, but Albert did not react to any of her little signals. Finally she gave up. Marie missed the young woman's visits, along with her tasty bread, for a long while.

When Cora came to live there, a totally different situation arose. Marie could not believe her eyes as she suddenly saw an Albert full of personality and good spirits. Her son, who was just past thirty, began mooning around like a callow love struck youth, causing Marie to float on air. Thankfully, Cora was equally smitten. After a whirlwind romance the pair married and the newlyweds happily lived with Marie for several years. The house was big enough that she gave the couple a whole floor to themselves. The arrangement worked out fine for the trio. Cora came to love Marie, as Marie loved her. She provided a great deal of help to the older woman in the daily chores associated with the boarding house. Years passed and no babies came. There were a couple of possible miscarriages and three sure ones. Another pregnancy resulted in a tragic stillbirth at seven months. Cora could not manage to carry a child to term, the one flaw in her life. Albert hurt because his wife was in such emotional agony. He would have liked to have children, but nothing was more important to him than his sweet Cora. If a choice were given to him, a child held no real importance when compared to his wife. He did not already know, or love, some possible child but Cora was the light in his life. If anyone chose to analyze Albert Rolande from a distance, *romantic* was the last quality that would have been attached to him. No question that he was a handsome man, but above all, his positive attributes were that he was solid, hard working, responsible, God-fearing and respectful. Albert had been unwilling to settle for less than his heart's desire in his search for a mate. When he met Cora, there was a single instant when his soul recognized hers as the one. Though children were a part of his original domestic dream, he was now afraid that Cora's health might be compromised and he could not bear that. Without her awareness, he had recently begun to take precautions. In his shaving kit was a supply of French letters. Cora never intruded into his personal toiletries, or his business papers. So his secret was safe. He felt badly about deceiving her, but he thought it best.

They had been married eight years when Sally came seeking a dressmaker. Two years before, Albert completed the building of the house himself. Both experienced mixed emotions moving away from his mother. Marie felt it to be the best solution because her concerns for Cora's health were the strongest of her emotions. Perhaps, she thought, getting away from the stairs and all the extra work might help her daughter-in-law. Without much effort, she found another island girl to help her in exchange for reduced rent.

Sally's newly rekindled relationship with her cousin filled a void in her life. Since Miss Valerie's death she cultivated no other close acquaintance. In all probability, her actions were unconsciously deliberate. If the tall fair woman did not take the time to create relationships, then she could not lose the people she came to love.

Over the next few months, Cora created exquisite clothing for Sally to wear. Her skills were such that the carriages of the white society women came rolling up to her door regularly. Cora utilized every bit of her talent and skill in the wardrobe she fashioned for Sally. Sally's long-legged body was the perfect natural foil for the new flapper styles. Cora enjoyed the design and sewing of well made clothing. Her craftsmanship was topnotch and she loved sewing for such a perfect figure. Sally looked forward to the days that she set aside time for her fittings, or to pick up garments. The cousins spent quiet times of enjoyment with conversations over tea and sandwiches. For some reason, Sally never brought her sons into the comfortably rekindled relationship. Cora often asked after them, but Sally always found some excuse not to bring her sons with her. She seemed to be guarding this time for herself.

Sally was envious of Cora's quiet, orderly life. Her cousin's world was centered in the spacious and well crafted Victorian cottage. She did her sewing, crafting and doll making in a lovely room designed for that purpose. Though Sally did own her house and the business, she envied the domestic bliss that belonged to Cora. Anyone could see the love shared by the Rolandes. Sally knew that if Bernard hadn't gone off to France and gotten himself killed, she would have had it too. Seldom did she allow herself to dwell on her dreadful turn of fortune, but from time to time she permitted her spirits to drop as low as possible. Doing anything else required more effort than she could summon.

The business consumed Sally, partly because it was the one place in her life without bad memories. The public's acceptance of her restaurant was prompt and wholehearted. In return she gave them superior food at a good value in a pleasant surrounding.

Fouchet's role continued beyond transferring the property. Valerie Broussard had spoken to him at length about her young friend. As part of the service to his client he had made sure that Mrs. Broussard's affection was not being compromised. The investigation had assured him that the girl was worthy of the marvelous gift she would one day receive. He also promised Valerie that he would continue to serve as the young woman's attorney if she desired. Sally had a good feeling about this man and shared her plans with him. Fouchet guided her in setting up all of the necessary business structures quietly and competently. Initially, few people were aware of the identity of the actual owner of the new restaurant. Sally hired a young man named Martin Jiles to assist her. 'Marteen', as he preferred to be called, acquired his experience in the business just as she did, by several years of hard work in a major French Quarter restaurant. Unlike Sally, he was a native of New Orleans. His manners and carriage were admirable. Like Sally he possessed extremely fair skin. Unlike his new boss, Martin felt that he was special because of the color of his complexion. If he had been a smidgen of a shade lighter, or just braver, without a doubt he would have quietly disappeared into the racial landscape of some far city. He might have been like Sally's cousin Geneva, a pretty gray-eyed blonde, who simply went away and let people treat her as she looked. The question of race never surfaced for her.

Despite his secret feelings, Martin thought Sally was the most amazing woman he had ever met. He admired the way that she ran her business, quietly keeping a very low profile. He understood most of her reasons. She allowed him to be the more visible person with the patrons, but anyone who worked there knew where the power lay. When the business was getting started, Sally worked as hard as any person in her kitchen. She had been seen to scrub dishes, cook or mop, equally often as those employed exclusively for those purposes. With the passage of time, her efforts at manual labor were required less often. However, she did often give her attention to the private dining rooms upstairs. These wealthy patrons were those who provided the priceless social influence that was the impetus for the success of the café. As the Prohibition Era continued to flourish, barriers began to lower. New Orleans simply maintained its tolerance for anyone who had the nerve to flout society. That a colored woman owned the successful enterprise became a non-issue. As the local society patrons became exposed to the beautiful young woman, she became a minor celebrity. Sally could care less about the celebrity, but she did understand that the cult of personality could make or break a restaurant. By late 1927, she had been the proprietor of *Café Petite Rouge* for two full years. It operated cleanly in the black.

When she started wearing the new clothes, she caused an immediate sensation. Cora had done a remarkable job. Because of the name of the establishment, they decided to make red her signature color. No less than five exquisite dresses in shades of red hung in her wardrobe closet. Since it was still a brave color for a lady in the Crescent City, everyone noticed. Sally remained the same low-key person inside, but her wardrobe elevated her to the status of local fashion icon in a short time. People who saw Sally Langlois stride around in her establishment were under the impression that her clothes were shipped from 'away'. Sally loved the clothing that Cora made for her. Her entire adult life had been focused on necessity. She did not splurge on anything. She used part of her initial inheritance to open the restaurant. However, more than two-thirds of the money remained untouched. When they moved into the house on Orleans Street, she spent a minimum amount adjusting the home to her family's needs.

Her wardrobe became the catalyst for Sally Langlois to pay attention to her own needs. Her appearance had always required little effort and upkeep because of her natural beauty. With the new clothing, she found the inclination to pamper herself a bit. She began to apply color to her lips, cheeks and knees in the fashion of the day. Her barely curled chestnut colored hair had hung below her shoulders in a lackluster fashion since childhood. Daringly, she allowed someone to sculpt it into one of the new bobbed coifs. The cut released a wave pattern that framed her face fetchingly. Her heavily lashed gray eyes became even more arresting. Sally was now one of the genuine exotic beauties for which New Orleans was renowned. The stark changes in her façade caught the attention of just about everyone who laid eyes on her, a full grown woman at the height of her glory.

6

Some of this particular group of well-dressed young colored men often came into *Café Petite Rouge*. Among the restaurants, diners and cafeterias around the Quarter, the group favored the tasty, ample fare of this cafe. Included in their midst tonight was someone who was newer to the scene. Michael Tolliver ended up down here in New Orleans by accident. In 1917, he had been one of a handful of colored college students at a small Jesuit university in upstate New York. When he came home and announced to his grandmother that he intended to join the Army, she fainted dead away. Her life's sole purpose, since his birth, had been keeping him safe. Now it was out of her control. His father, her only child, had been killed on a lonely road in Georgia when Michael was two years old. Supposedly the 'accident' was the result of being run over by a hit and run driver. The Dixie authorities refused to associate his father's death with the repeatedly warnings given to him by some good local gents about his 'uppity ways'. Michael's mother and grandmother had taken him and fled north hastily. Margaret, his mother, caught pneumonia the first winter and died. The older woman always said that her real cause of death was a broken heart. His grandmother treated Michael like royalty as he grew up, a child loved fiercely and almost to the point of reverence.

Over the years she worked as a domestic for one of the finest families in New York City. She began her employment as a live-in general domestic worker, then began cooking after the cook needed help for a particularly big dinner. A sweet older woman named Mamie, she enlisted Carrie Tolliver to assist her with some of the basic tasks that night. Carrie did this while still handling her own chores and proved herself capable. In the large busy household, the duties ended up continuing and expanding. Carrie encountered no problems running the household efficiently. In addition, her tasty contributions to the meals were noticed. When the woman died a year later, Carrie seamlessly moved into the top spot with little fanfare. Other workers were hired to assist her as needed. The employer simply increased her pay and spoke to her directly about their needs. Her employment in the household had continued to now.

During Michael's childhood she used every opportunity to obtain the good will and influence of these people on his behalf. She was merciless in her efforts. Any chance that she could create to showcase her precious and precocious orphaned grandchild was used to the maximum effect. The family got to know the handsome little brown boy and salved their genuine sense of social consciousness by providing him with help whenever possible. Michael was the beneficiary of his grandmother's very deliberate campaign to make every opportunity available to him. Each ounce of strength that Carrie Tolliver could muster was used to provide for Michael. On her days off, she sometimes worked through an agency cooking for banquets. Any personal life was sacrificed on the altar of her determination that Michael's life would never be like her son's had been. He would have good schools and then music lessons, just like the white children did.

She found that the church pianist was an accomplished piano teacher. When the woman told her that Michael possessed considerable talent for music, Carrie was elated. The original idea had simply been to give him exposure to the many things she wished she could have given his father. Her son had basically taught himself to play on the old upright piano in the church back home. He had been a good son, and an extremely proud young man. Carrie was convinced that though her son's pride had caused his own tragic death, her grandson was going to have a chance at a life he could be proud of.

Her plan was going along just fine. The judge that she worked for helped to open doors, but Michael used his ability and intelligence to sail through them all. He got into the schools and excelled. When he was admitted to that university upstate, Carrie was certain that her battle had been won. The boy would go on to be a man of substance, maybe a doctor or lawyer. There was a lot of room for colored professionals here in the north. She had not counted on the Kaiser to upset her applecart of dreams.

The young men at Michael's university began enlisting before the United States entered the war. Some of them had gone to Canada to do so. He knew that Carrie would object, so he delayed his own enlistment until he graduated from the university mid-year. Finally in February he went down to the recruitment office. His timing was blessed. After his initial training, he ended up being shipped to Des Moines, Iowa. The training there was rigorous and sometimes racist, but in June 1917, he was commissioned as one of the first colored officers in the U.S. Army. His intelligence, good looks and college education made him a natural for this new corps. Despite her previous protests, Carrie was overwhelmed when she saw the newly commissioned First Lieutenant Michael Tolliver in his dress uniform. Even his anxious grandmother could not help but acknowledge that here was a fine figure of a man. Michael received orders assigning him to the 803rd Pioneer Infantry and was immediately shipped to France.

The easy camaraderie among the servicemen was something that Michael came to cherish. Among the elite corps of recruits were well-educated young colored men from all over the country. During much of Michael's life, his associations with others his age had been very restricted. In her zeal to protect her grandson, Carrie Tolliver consistently limited his exposure to his peers. Here he made friends easily and promptly. He developed a close friendship with another young officer who was assigned to the battalion's band.

Jefferson Arnaud seemed to be Michael's direct opposite. Michael's behavior and personality were as crisp and sharp as the temperatures on any northern winter morning. Jeff's southern roots saturated every part of him. His movements were as languid and smooth as his speech was syrupy. The matinee idol good looks were only the first key to his charm. His golden aquiline features and dreamy eyes were a product of the Creole contribution to his bloodline. When the French Mademoiselles caught on that he actually understood a great deal of their chatter, he had to swat them away. While he was just as tall as Michael, his body was whippet thin and deceptive. Many a fellow misread his graceful physique to be frail, but subsequently found his strength to be steel-like in nature.

Jeff loved clothing in a way that Michael did not understand, constantly raving about some tailor on Royal Street back at home in New Orleans. Of course, he referred to the address as 'Rue Royal'. He took every spare moment given to him in Paris, to shop. Roaming about the streets of the City of Lights, Jeff felt almost at home. Not only did he appreciate the clothing, but also much of the food was distinctly familiar. Here, he could obtain the golden, crusty loaves of bread and rich pastries that he had eaten all of his life. Jeff easily acquired the palate for virtually every sumptuous item on the average French menu.

Along with clothing and food, Jefferson Arnaud loved his music. Included in his belongings, was a vintage saxophone that he had owned since he was twelve years old. Only the exquisite muted patina betrayed its age. Like any lovingly treasured thing, it barely exhibited a single scratch. Its battered and beaten black leather case bore the bruises inflicted over the years. This saxophone seemed to be a natural extension of Jeff's body, as it was usually in his hand and at his lips during off duty hours. Many of the colored soldiers in the bands got together at night and played informally. The sweet melodic wail of Jeff's sax could be heard in these casual jam sessions. His unique patterns of rhythm easily distinguished themselves. This, too, increased his status with the locals, since these jam sessions sometimes found their way into the clubs. Because Jazz was all the rage in Paris, Jeff became a minor celebrity. His good looks, charm and skill with the language, when combined with his musical talent were a completely devastating package for the local females. He was never without feminine companionship, and was a point of envy of the majority of the service men. Michael did not feel the same way.

Jeff teased Michael because of his lackluster interest in the nubile young French females. Unlike his friend, Michael did not think of all women as his possible conquests, nor did he treat them in such a manner. Carrie's teachings and example had shaped the New Yorker's attitudes about women. Unlike most of the young men who had found themselves far away from home for the first time, Michael did not abandon the values given to him. Jeff had always been a ladies' man and things were no different here because the sophisticated French readily accepted his attitudes and behavior. Still, Michael feared that something unsavory would happen to his friend at any moment. Combat seemed to be the lesser threat. With the grace of God, both men made it through the war unscathed physically. The horrific toll of humanity around them did, however, mar them emotionally. For each of them, friendship was a salvation.

While Michael returned stateside immediately after discharge, Jeff lingered in Paris for a bit. He capitalized on his established celebrity and considered remaining in Europe. Ultimately, he became homesick. Before going home to New Orleans, he stopped to visit for a month with Michael in New York. His charm worked equally well on Grandma Carrie as it had done on the Mademoiselles. She tried everything in her cook's bag of tricks to fatten up Michael's friend. Jeff fooled her by eating everything that she put on his plate and never gaining an ounce.

Michael and Jeff spent their time roaming the streets of the city. It was a different place for Michael now. Though he had spent his initial time back home investigating career possibilities and networking with old college friends, his friend's arrival diluted his focus. With Jeff in tow, he discovered another side of the city he had grown up in. Having saved virtually every dime of his pay over the period of his enlistment, Michael consciously chose to take his time making up his mind about the future. After his discharge from the Army, his original thought was to board a train and go west to California, simply because it was a different arena. He had heard much about the West Coast area. When he left New York with his friend, his intention was to do a quick tourist's stop in the Crescent City. His thought that he would see the French Quarter and the Jazz spots and then be on his way, proved to be a fallacy. The easy rhythms of the delta city seeped under his skin. Michael only knew the high energy of New York City. Not surprisingly New Orleans' sensual spirit caught him totally unaware. In some ways, it reminded him of Paris and he began to understand why Jeff had felt so at home there. The lazy local rhythm captivated and then captured him. When they were overseas, he had fallen into playing with the group of musicians with whom Jeff played. So when it was discovered that the group's previous piano man had skipped off to the Chicago jazz scene, naturally Jeff drew Michael in to join in on the sessions with his local group. Drawing on his Parisian exposure, Jeff was able to keep the group booked constantly.

The northerner began to love everything about the New Orleans jazz scene. After the jam sessions the men found themselves prowling the after hours joints and speakeasies. Michael discovered that he had an affinity for gambling. It seemed as though Lady Luck had became his constant companion and paramour. His stay stretched from days to weeks, then months, until one day he realized that he had begun to consider this place home. Some of Jeff's love of luxury crossed over into his consciousness.

The Royal street tailors knew him well now. Michael Tolliver was a man discovering new facets of himself. His looks, his attitudes and his sensibilities had undergone a metamorphosis.

7

Four, of the usual five, musicians decided to have a decent meal before they set out for tonight's club date. The bass player recommended the café as a very good place to eat. So far, they were heartily enjoying their meals. An easy jocular conversation bandied back and forth. Then Sally came walking slowly down from the private dining rooms. Instead of one of her red garments, tonight she wore a dark silver bias cut chemise dress with an uneven hem. The smoky colored shimmering fabric undulated with her every movement in an almost liquid manner. Compared to the softly lit dining room, the chandelier highlighted the staircase like a spotlight. As she descended the open, gently curving flight of steps, her long and elegantly shapely legs were what caught Michel's eye first. As he raised his glance, the rest of her exquisite body followed. By the time that he looked directly into her smoke colored eyes, he was absolutely in awe of her beauty. He was not alone in his reverie. Conversation at the table ceased completely. Jeff was the first one to recover.

"I don't know about y'all, but from what I see, it's rather obvious that over there must lie the stairway to heaven."

His gentle drawl was accompanied by a one sided smile. The other men laughed nervously, as if he had read their minds. Only the bass player had been unaware, since he was seated with his back toward the stairway. He turned quickly to look when the New Yorker spoke.

"If so, I believe that the inhabitants are definitely deserting the premises. Who is that woman?" Michael's baritone voice sounded stunned.

His observation shocked the other men. Never was he the one to even comment about women. The group often wondered what it would take to cause a reaction from him. His calm demeanor was clearly shattered. Rising from the table, he took his napkin in hand and placed it on the table beside his plate in one economical motion. Before Sally reached the door to the kitchen, Michael was beside her. She carried a crystal tray filled with a matching decanter and glasses. The tall handsome man startled her as he opened the door smoothly. He appeared out of nowhere. Sally looked up at him with curiosity and dismissed him in the same few seconds.

"Thank you, sir."

She was through the door without a backward glance, leaving Michael standing in a frozen position as if he were the kitchen sentinel. After a few moments he realized that he needed to know about her, to know her. When she did not emerge after a few minutes, his first urge was to follow her through the door. Then it occurred to him that he might cause her some kind of trouble with her employer. Looking around he saw the man at the counter in the front entry area, Martin Jiles. Without pausing, he approached him. Martin recognized Michael as a part of a group of musicians who frequented the café. While he understood that the men enjoyed some measure of local celebrity, they only existed on his personal radar because they were good customers. Martin was a snob of a sort common in 20th century New Orleans. In his eyes, the young man was very well dressed and undeniably handsome, but in a dark sort of way. When he spoke, Martin also observed that he was a definite outsider, a northerner at that. He resented everything about the man in front of him.

"Excuse me, sir. I was hoping that you could assist me."

Michael thinking to put his best foot forward, smiled to impress.

"Yes, what is it?" Martin angled his blond flecked eyebrows in an arrogant, quizzical manner.

"I was wondering about the identity of the young lady who just went into the kitchen. Could you please tell me her name? She looks like someone that I…."

Michael struggled to come up with a rational reason for his interest.

"I'm sorry. I have no idea to whom you refer." Martin turned away from the man. A scowl marred his cow-licked forehead. The pale color of the edges of his hairline took away the definition, making him look older.

Michael controlled the anger that began to suffuse his being. Some of these southern whites were unbearable. New Orleans was a little more relaxed than the tales that he had heard from his grandmother about Georgia, but still there was no denying that the color lines were enforced when desired here. He turned to walk back to the table. Maybe the girl was white, French or Italian with a tan. Maybe that was why the man took such an attitude. The racial lines were so blurry here that it was sometimes hard to tell. He hadn't thought that she could be white, or

Cajun but maybe he was wrong. She was fair, but he sensed some kinship. As he sat back down at the table, he was very quiet.

Jeff was the first one to speak. He chuckled as he cut into the plump, juicy stuffed pork chops.

"My man, I have never seen you act so aggressively. But I must admit that she is an absolute gem. Did you have any luck?"

"I don't know. The white guy probably didn't want his help..."

The bass player cut him off.

"That guy is not white, first of all."

Michael always noticed that some of the local accent came out in some words sounding very much the same as some of the New York accents, especially Brooklyn. *First*, came out "*fuist*". What the man said began to sink in.

"Marty Jiles lives uptown near my lady friend, Janette and I guarantee you that he is the help. Hey, I just ignore him and his attitude. It's his personal problem. But I have seen the sweetheart before. The rumor is that she is the actual owner of the place… real low key, except for her looks. Her name is Sally. Last name is something French-y."

Jeff cut in. "Ham, now remember… half of New Orleans is *somethin' French-y.*"

Michael loved the way that the natives referred to their city as "N'Awlins". It became one word by a graceful diphthong.

Hambone Williams, the bass player, laughed as he finished up his meal. The big man ate with genuine enjoyment.

"Man, you are so right, yea. Yo' French-y ass ought to know. Yea! But anyway, my girl says she used to work with this woman at a hotel a few years ago. One night I brought her here to eat and she caught a glimpse of her, too. We waited round, but she never came out again. How she got from there to here, I don't know. But I believe my lady."

"So she is beautiful and mysterious. Michael, maybe Hambone can find out something more about her. Gentlemen, we need to be on our way. We have a well paid gig tonight."

Jeff rose from the table and waved the others away as he placed the money for the meals and a tip.

Michael tarried to be the last to leave the table. With an almost desperate deliberation, he glanced back toward the kitchen as he turned to go. Like a sweet apparition that he summoned, the tall woman appeared through the doors and mounted the stairs. He had never seen anyone quite like her before, but he determined that he would see her again.

Michael made the conclusion that if the woman were the owner of the establishment a good chance existed that she would be there prior to opening. It might also be a means to avoid the overly protective man from the front desk. He would make it his business to be nearby to seek her out very soon. Though Michael Tolliver tried to tell himself that he would be in no real rush to find her, inside his heart of hearts, he felt compelled to make the connection. The very next day he was up and dressed much earlier than usual because he abandoned the late night card game. In record time he was parked near the little café.

When he saw that it seemed he would be in New Orleans for at least awhile, Michael purchased one of the new Ford automobiles. It came in handy to get around with the musicians. His sense of discipline made it natural for him to handle the transport. Besides, the sleek black machine appealed to all of his awakened senses.

He arrived at the end of the block around three o'clock. The establishment opened at six in the evening daily and always had a good dinner crowd. The post midnight closing time allowed them to catch the 'after' crowds. Society people arrived after the opera, or after balls. Everyone came either before or after a night carousing the clubs and speakeasies. The crowds were diverse in every possible way. All decent people who could afford the price of the meal walked through the door. Now Michael sat quietly and watched the employees begin to arrive. When the cleaning crew tidied the outside areas, he glanced up to see the woman in a window upstairs. He could not figure out how she could have gotten past him. It then occurred to him that just maybe she had already been inside. Or there was the possibility that she had come in by a different door. He drove around the block and saw that there was another obscure entrance near the back corner. He would remember that. Then it occurred to him that he could just go up and ask for the proprietor. Even if it wasn't successful, there was always a chance. He drove back to the front entrance and walked up to the door. Just as he was about to knock, the door opened.

She walked up to the door, opened it and stopped in her tracks. Her first thought was that it was another nuisance suitor. But this man was somehow different, a cut above the usual. He was extremely well dressed and well-built. This was apparent since her eyes first hit his broad shoulders, encased in an extremely well-cut tweed jacket. As her field of vision moved up to his handsome face, she saw his lush mustache, the edges of his sleekly pomaded hair and recognized him as the door opening man from the night before. Atop his head was a sporty tweed cap matching the jacket.

"The café is not yet open, sir." The soft drawl in her voice thrilled him. He loved the "h" sound substituted for "r".

"Yes, I am aware of that, Miss. I came here in hopes of meeting you."

Michael had removed his cap respectfully and placed it in his hands.

"My name is Michel Tolliver and I believe that we need to meet."

For some reason that even she did not consciously understand, Sally did not respond with her usual negativity. Martin Jiles came up just as she was about to reply. He grasped immediately that the man was the jazz musician from the night before. Thinking that he should leap to his employer's assistance, he spoke quickly to the man.

"Sir, I believe that you need to move along. We are not yet open for business." He did not see that Sally was not at all irritated. She turned calmly toward him instead.

"Don't worry, Martin. Everything here is just fine. Please go on inside."

Her manner dismissed him and she turned back to the tall stranger. Martin slunk inside as fast as possible. His feelings were very hurt and confused. The reddened color suffusing his face told the story. Sally never dealt with such people before.

"Well, Mr. Michael Tolliver, I appreciated your courteous actions on last evening. My name is Sally Langlois. Why exactly do we 'need' to know one another?"

There was a humorous undertone to her voice. A smile flashing across her face was all the encouragement that Michael needed. He pled his case. He was new to the city and he knew so few people. Every excuse that he could compose came spilling from his mouth. He had never done such a thing. The few women with whom he had been involved, had approached him. Somehow, women just hadn't been a priority until now. For some reason that she couldn't consciously fathom, Sally heard herself agree to have dinner with him on the next evening. The catch was that it would be upstairs in her establishment. She assured him that it would be like any other regular social engagement. He could order the food and pay the bill. Sally had learned to always be a solid businesswoman first.

After the man named Michael Tolliver walked to his car and drove away, Sally stood for a moment, stunned. What had she been thinking? A warm flush of embarrassment crept up her neck to her cheeks. For all these years alone, she had been careful about such liberties. It was hard sometimes, but her conclusion was that relationships were not for her. Virtually all of her feelings about the opposite sex had begun and ended with Bernard. Maybe it was time to forgive him for dying and let go. She shook off her uncertainty and opened the door to her building. Just maybe she could have a fresh start. This man from up north might be the chance that she needed.

8

On the following morning Sally woke up with a smile on her face. For the first time in a long while, she had something new in her life to consider, to ponder and dream about. She liked the look of the tall northerner. His crisp, no nonsense speech was exciting. When she stood watching him walk to his car on the previous afternoon, she noticed his elegant carriage and physique. Everything that she saw suggested a disciplined, structured person. Sally definitely wanted to learn more about him. Her day progressed at its usual pace despite her underlying anticipation.

When she left for the restaurant that day, her thoughts focused on which dresses she would pull from the dressing room closet upstairs. Finally, the choice was a beaded dress of a rich mustard color for which she actually had a matching pair of spoon-heeled slippers. Cora had made sure that all of the dresses were properly accessorized. Most dresses had hats, bags and some wraps coordinated to them. Her cousin created a complete wardrobe for Sally, a real luxury for someone who previously rarely paid serious attention to her clothing. The gold colored dress would be absolutely right, its color especially flattering to her skin tones in candlelight.

Michael, meanwhile, was more concerned about the evening than Sally was. Choosing a suit to wear had taken him over an hour. He changed his mind about a shirt and tie several times, while the choice of cufflinks took almost as long. It suddenly occurred to him that his behavior on this specific occasion must be worse than that of Jefferson Arnaud. Such vanity was tiring, but he dearly wanted each aspect of the evening to be perfect including his own sense of comfort. He thought that her decision to have dinner in her own café was interesting. Certainly it meant that she could control the entire event and feel more at ease. Something suggested to him that she was totally about control. He was perfectly willing to allow her that privilege.

Strong women were all that Michael had ever known. For a brief time he had been infatuated with a very pretty girl from church, though ultimately he tired of her. Eyelashes and dimples were the sum of her substance, bringing him to decide that sweet was not his cup of tea. Luckily, she tired of the distance between them during his college years. Despite the relatively short span of highway, he did not feel compelled to return to the city even twice a month to see her. He was so happy when she wrote that she hoped he could forgive her, but… It was clear that his grandmother liked that girl, Francie, a lot. Of course Carrie had not been the one to hold her in an embrace. Something was decidedly missing in her, Michael felt. Even though she went through the motions, her body seemed lifeless, as if the passion was an act. He sensed that this Louisiana woman was composed of steelier stuff, despite the exquisite exterior. Hambone had told him all that his lady friend knew about Sally Langlois. It was just enough to truly stir his curiosity.

After arriving at the restaurant, Sally jotted some notes for the staff. First on her list was the set-up of her favorite dining room upstairs. The room contained an antique chandelier that originally hung in an antebellum mansion up the river. When she spotted it in the salvage yard, she could hardly believe her luck. Cleaning it up and restoring it took an enormous amount of work, but when it was finally installed, the results were clearly well worth the effort. Whenever a patron was important or just well liked, this was the room she most often gave to them.

Tonight for the first time, she would be both the hostess and client in this room herself. Once she was dressed, she saw that her detailed instructions had been followed to a '*t*'. A magnificent array of fresh flowers sat on the mahogany sideboard, as well as the table. Silver gleamed in the candlelight. Sally loved the simple dignity of the fine white linen and china. Here she wanted the food to take center stage, not the place settings. Satisfied that all was as it should be, Sally withdrew to her office. Martin had been instructed to show Michael upstairs upon his arrival. She saw the stern expression that he unsuccessfully attempted to wipe from his face. It was apparent that he disapproved of the northerner, but Sally could care less. The last thing that she ever worried about was someone else's approval of her life choices. Besides, Martin was such an old lady. He could have been a decent looking man, though a bit pale for her personal taste, but he was missing some key ingredient. Sally did not care to speculate what that might be.

Michael strode confidently into the restaurant. He wore a fine wool gabardine suit of a pale taupe color. The dark gold silk tie was an ideal touch. Martin Jiles examined the tall man disdainfully. He hated to admit it, but the stranger wore a very well tailored suit of clothing, and wore it well. He wondered if the man had purchased it locally. After all, New Orleans did offer fine clothing for gentlemen. It was clear that there was nothing he could do about Sally's choices, so he accepted that limitation, and was thankful that at least he appeared to be someone with good taste. Since the man might be around the establishment, he wouldn't be a complete embarrassment.

When Martin knocked softly on Sally's office door, she was initially startled. This was new territory for her. Maybe it wouldn't go past one dinner. She took a deep breath and rose to open the door. Martin informed her that her guest was seated in the dining room with a menu as she had requested. Thanking him, she took a final cursory glance in the mirror and walked down the hallway. Michael sat patiently with the menu in hand. He rose when she entered and pulled out her chair. It was such a temptation to him to kiss her cheek in greeting. His decision was to take no chances, so he brought her hand up to his lips instead.

"Good evening, Mr. Tolliver. I see that you are prompt. That is a quality to admire in a man."

She smiled as she made the statement, so he wasn't sure if she was serious. He had been exactly on time. Carrie had instilled this in him since childhood and his military service reinforced it.

"Yes, I believe so. If nothing else, a man can be on time. It is the first test that you are a man of your word. I am a man of my word." He looked directly into her eyes as he spoke.

"I believe that the same applies to women, sir. So let's say that we are people of our word. I don't believe that character traits can be restricted to being male or female."

Sally knew that she might as well test his mettle here and now. So many men had strange beliefs about women. He was quiet for a moment. She wondered if it was over before it had a chance to begin. When he spoke, she knew that he was special.

"I've never thought about saying it that way before, but you are absolutely right. My grandmother would certainly agree. You see she raised me alone and she was a hard taskmaster. She provided me with every opportunity that she could beg, borrow, or steal." He chuckled softly, but his expression was a bit nostalgic. Sally saw that he sincerely cherished his grandmother. This was certainly a good sign.

"Is she still alive? And where did you grow up?"

"Oh, Carrie Tolliver is alive and kicking in New York, New York. She and my mother took me there from Georgia after my father's death. I was only two years old at the time. My mother did not make it past the first winter. My grandma is all that I know."

"You were an only child?" Sally sensed some connection here.

"Yes, I was. It never bothered me. I was kept busy."

She believed that he was probably a decent person. There was so much more to learn about him. Most frightening for her was discussing her own life. How would he feel about her having children? It was going to be a long evening.

"Have you decided on the menu choices yet? We have wonderful food."

"Yes, I must agree with you. I have actually eaten here several times with great satisfaction."

As he thought about it, he decided to take a chance. He folded the menu and put it aside. He might learn some things about her this way.

"Why don't you make the choices? I am open to new experiences. You are clearly the expert here."

Pulling the bell chord, Sally was delighted to take charge. The waiter who came in was a bit surprised to see her. Miss Sally didn't make it a practice to have guests. He was determined to give her the best service he could provide for more than one reason. She was such a decent young woman and she deserved a life. He, like the rest of her loyal staff, often speculated about the reasons why she did not seem to have a real personal life despite the attention that she obviously received.

The meal was a resounding success. Michael savored every bite, more so than he had any other meal. He wondered if the food was really that tasty, or if it was the company. A good conversationalist, she spoke knowledgeably about food, her business, and life in general. Questions about his experiences living in a city like New York were peppered throughout. His ears loved the rich, sultry tone of her voice which, when coupled with the regional drawl was undeniably musical. He could listen to her speak for hours on end. However flattered he was that she was curious about him, Michael soon realized that Sally avoided giving clues about her self. He was determined to get to know this woman, so he began a direct approach.

"Sally, did you grow up here in New Orleans?"

Her reply was prompt enough.

"No, I am a country girl. I grew up in St John Parish. It lies north of here. It was, is, a very rural area. I moved here several years ago."

She looked directly at him as she spoke. The candlelight flickered in her gray eyes. He could tell that there was more to the story. Was she going to let him into her life? He persisted.

"Do you still have family there?"

He didn't want to make her feel that he was prying, but everything about her was of interest to him. Sally decided that he would have to find out her story sooner or later. She plunged ahead.

"My father lives there still. In fact, he lives in the house that my great grandfather and his brothers built. There are no sisters or brothers, though." She paused. "Michael, I don't know how you will feel about this, but I have two sons, Bernard and Antoine."

She stopped abruptly and looked down at her hands. Michael saw that she wore no rings. He asked the next logical question.

"Are you married?"

He didn't know if he wanted to know the answer, even as he asked the question. If she said yes, then hc knew that he wouldn't see her again. If the answer was no, he didn't know what to think.

"I was, once upon a time. My husband, Bernard, was killed in France."

Her eyes remained fixed on her hands. Michael had to restrain himself from making a loud sigh of relief. He hadn't considered that possibility. He also hadn't thought about someone else's children. They could take it one step at a time.

"I am so very sorry. It must have been hard for you. I ended up as a Captain in the Army. I served in France, so I have some idea of how awful it was."

Sally looked up at him. He sounded sincere, but he couldn't possibly understand. Her reply was measured and solemn.

"It was awful because he should never have left us to go in the first place. I loved him with all my heart. My life has not been the same."

Michael saw the deeply felt pain in her eyes, heard it in her voice. He remembered stories that his grandmother told him about his mother having actually died of a broken heart. He also knew that Carrie Tolliver's one love was Thomas Tolliver, his grandfather who died a few years before his father had been killed. Undoubtedly, in front of him sat another woman who suffered mightily from a broken heart. He did not know if he was man enough to help her heal, but he was willing to try. He gently took her face in his hands.

"Sally, we have to release our pain if we are ever to heal. That much my grandmother drilled into my head. She was a big believer in trying to move on. I know that this does not directly relate to you, but my father was murdered, shortly after his father had died tragically in an accident. He was her only child and she said that she had to make the hard decision that she could not dwell on any of it or it would have killed everything good inside of her. She has repeated many times over the years that my mother did allow it to kill her. Your husband did not want to leave you. Even though I didn't know him, I know that. I can feel that you loved him a great deal. I know that he would have loved you in return. No man in his right mind would ever want to leave a woman like you."

Large tears rolled down her face. She suddenly felt very stupid. What was she doing? She hardly knew this man and here she was pouring out her soul. She stood up and walked over to the sideboard.

"I am so sorry. I have ruined the evening. Michael, I don't normally talk about my personal life. I guess now I know why." After wiping her eyes with a handkerchief retrieved from the drawer, she looked up apologetically. Michael stood up, covered the space in a step and gently put his hands around her shoulders. His voice was as absolutely sincere as his smile was touching.

"Sally, the evening is not ruined. We are new friends learning about one another. I now know that your eyes are even more beautiful when they leak because they look silver."

They both laughed and sat down. She thought that he was probably the nicest man that she had ever met. And she was glad that she had met him. After dabbing with the square of linen again, she looked up and forced a smile.

"I promise you that they are now repaired. Let's have dessert. The pecan pie is my own contribution to the meal."

This particular dining room included a casual seating area with a chaise, an elegant stained glass floor lamp and a small carved fruitwood table. She pulled the tassel of the heavy gold bell chord, went to the sideboard and removed a silver covered dish. When the waiter came, he brought a silver pot filled with pungent fresh coffee. Michael had developed a taste for the aromatic chicory-laced coffee served here. It was the perfect counter to the opulent sweetness of the pecan pie. He teased her about that dessert.

"Do you really expect me to believe that you cooked this with your own two precious hands?"

"Of course. Don't forget, Michael. I am a real country girl. My mother and Mama' started teaching me to cook practically as soon as I learned to walk. My grandmother was especially serious about making sure that I knew 'the womanly arts'. She's the inspiration for the name of my café."

Michael considered it for a moment. His knowledge of French was at least rudimentary. The meaning of the words was clear, but he didn't quite understand their significance.

"The little red café, right?"

"Yes, she spoke patois as much as English. Her nickname for me was *mon petite rouge*. My hair was bright red as a child. It has faded a great deal since."

"My little red? Oh, okay now I get it. You must have been an absolute knockout." He put the picture in his mind.

"I don't know about all of that. I was kind of a big, long legged tomboy." She laughed and shook her head is disbelief.

He looked down at her crossed legs pointedly. There was no way she could ever have been a tomboy. He had never seen a woman anywhere who was more gorgeous, or feminine. Her features were so softly pretty. This was what made her so striking. The contrast of the large doe shaped gray eyes and sweetly full lips to the pale skin made her so striking. There was nothing sharp about her face.

He did not want to insult her, or move too fast. But they were both adults and she was so desirable. He leaned forward and kissed her lips gently. Sally saw the kiss coming and did not avoid it. It had been a long time since she had allowed herself the sweet luxury of even a kiss.

"You are certainly no tomboy now, Sally."

"I don't feel like one with you around." She murmured.

"I should be going now. It was a beautiful evening. I hope that you will allow me the pleasure of seeing you again."

He halfway hoped that she would stop him from leaving. Though he was not looking for just a moment's thrill, at the moment he might be weak enough to think about settling. He put his arms around her and kissed her again. Sally drew her hand up between them and touched his face.

"It was lovely. Yes, I will be glad to see you again."

She stood and started clearing the small table. For the first time he noticed the dress that she wore. He sat for a few seconds and surveyed her from head to toe. 'God', he thought. 'What a precious package she is', and without question, he wanted the whole package. He stood and walked over to the door.

"I should say good night. I will be in touch shortly."

Touching his arm lightly, she took him to the back stairway. This time she kissed him quickly before she closed the door. Michael could not believe this turn of fate. Treasure had appeared when he least expected it. It had been his belief that he would find the right woman one day. However, he had mistakenly believed that somehow it would happen when he was ready to search for that woman. But here she was, everything that a man could possibly want in a woman. She was smart enough to run a successful business and her beauty threatened to stop his heart as well. There was no question that he would remain here in New Orleans now. Fate had presented an interesting new possibility.

On this Sunday evening he had no specific place to go after their dinner engagement. He felt on top of the world. The group had no scheduled gig, but maybe he could catch some of his cronies in an impromptu session. Michael drove a few blocks to one of the private clubs. As he thought, everyone was there. The group sat refreshing themselves between sets. Practically as soon as he entered, Jeff spotted him and beckoned him up to the bandstand. As he settled himself at the piano, Jeff came over, glass in hand, unable to control his curiosity.

"So, how did it go?" He barely contained himself. Because Jeff had stopped to visit earlier in the afternoon, Michael reluctantly ended up telling him about his dinner engagement. Clothes had been strewn about and Jeff knew immediately that something special was on the horizon. Michael didn't take that kind of time considering his clothing under normal circumstances. Jeff picked at him until Michael had virtually no choice but to explain. Now his friend was picking at him again much to his dismay.

With a sly smile and a chuckle he pressed for details.

"So, how was your evening? Is she everything that you expected?" He rattled the ice cubes in the glass.

"It was very nice. She is a lovely lady." Michael was tight lipped.

"Don't give me that line, my friend." Jeff spoke quietly, with an amused expression. "You forget who you are talking to, Michael. I am your old friend from the war. Your grandmother trusted me to care for you down here."

By now Michael was laughing at his friend's behavior. Jeff had no mercy. Anyone would have sworn that they were schoolboys. He really did not care to discuss the details of his evening, especially here and now. His time with Sally had been a precious promise.

"Can it, Jeff! You are so totally full of it! What ever happened to the gentlemen's code? The evening was completely wonderful. The lady is very special. We are not adolescent boys. That's all you get."

Turning away from Jeff, he began to pick out a melody. Jeff realized that Michael meant business. Returning to his spot, he put down the glass and answered his friend with a riff on his sax. In the time that he had known Michael, he had not seen this level of interest in any woman. Of course he received his share of attention from them, but this was the first time he saw that look in Michael's eyes. For some reason, he was irritated.

9

As usual her first task on Monday was balancing the previous week's books. Sally was in her office when Martin came up the stairs and knocked at her door.

"Come in, Martin." She recognized his tap. He came inside smiling.

"Hello. This was just delivered."

He handed her a large bouquet of flowers and a narrow rectangular package. A delighted Sally saw that the flowers were from *Leoni's,* the same florist that she used for the café. Though she was reasonably sure that the exquisite bouquet was from Michael, opening the attached card confirmed it. She wondered if he had chosen the flowers himself. Perhaps it was just the luck of the draw, however they were very special. But, she wondered, what was in the weighty box. When she opened the vellum box, she recognized the jeweler's sticker used as a closure. Inside was first a bulky object enclosed in fine tissue. The delicately crafted silver bracelet was beyond lovely, as well as undoubtedly expensive by her standards. As she held it against her wrist and admired the look of it, she had to admit that it was nice. There was no question that he would have spent entirely too much money on anything purchased at that particular store. Beneath the tissue was an envelope that included a note and a check. He had written, "*Never let it be said that I forget my debts. In the excitement of the moment, I missed the matter of my check. When I saw this bracelet I knew that your wrist was the place that it deserved to be. Besides, the silver is exactly the same shade as your eyes when they leak.*"

It was signed simply, "*M.T.*" Sally couldn't help but laugh. She had told him that he would be responsible for paying for the meal. It had been forgotten as quickly as she had said it. One thing was sure. So far he was a man of his word. The bracelet was another matter. Sally questioned the idea of expensive jewelry as a present after one date. He had been the perfect gentleman. This was turning out to be far more complicated than she had expected. Heck, she didn't even know what the rules were because her experience was so limited. She was a country girl and his background was so different. In the years that she had been alone, there had been one very brief, furtive fling. She had never even let that man into her real life. The physical loneliness had finally just gotten the best of her. She had been stretched so thinly… trying to get the business ready to open… adjusting to the loss of Miss Valerie. It had been overwhelming. The man had been the finish carpenter working on the remodeling. They ended up late in the same place together too often. Afterwards, she found it impossible to deal with the shame. For the first time, she experienced a purely physical attraction for a man. Eddie was his name, an extremely handsome and physical creature. She could remember that his thighs were elongated and well developed, like Bernard's had been. The heavy fabric of his pant legs strained against those rippling muscles. When she dropped some books going up the stairs, he helped her gather them. The incidental touch electrified them both. He had followed her up the stairs. Sally's face colored even now as she recalled the passionate intensity of the month long encounter. She was gripped by fear that everyone around could sense the sexual tension between the two of them. In fact she was sure that her father did figure it out. One night after the boys were in bed, they sat at the kitchen table sharing the last cup of coffee.

"The building is going just fine. Don't you think?" He asked. She was enjoying the coffee and the peace. Her days were usually too long between the job she continued to hold onto, some quick time with her sons, then nights checking progress at the site.

"Yes, Papa. I am very happy with the progress. Opening should be right about our original schedule. Next week, I'll draw up my menus and order form for the supply house. The week after that I am going to give my notice at the hotel."

"Sally, you work entirely too hard for such a young woman. Don't you think that it's time for you to start thinking about yourself a little more? I don't mean to pry into your business. I mean, you are full grown and all." He stammered a bit.

"Papa, I am thinking 'bout myself and these two boys that I've got to raise. They need to eat. And they grow out of shoes every week, it seems. You know a good pair of shoes costs $ 2.00 now? And don't even mention clothing."

"You need to worry about more than money, Sally. Bernard has been gone a long while now. Why don't you have a man in your life? A woman needs a man in her life."

"Papa, most of these men are not looking for a woman with two children attached. I am all that these boys have left."

A variety of images barreled through her mind. First of all, she thought about the assignations with Eddie. She knew that her father liked him a lot. Maybe… Oh God! Had her Papa found out something? She was so ashamed.

"Look here, I am doing just fine. I never want to have to worry about having enough money to care for my children. Maybe one day soon…" She looked down into the cup to hide the flush of her face. Under no circumstances did she wish to talk to him about this. One thing she knew absolutely, this was the end of Eddie. In her mind, he was not a Bernard.

Sally now recalled the conversation. Her father probably still worried about her, but he'd never again commented about her personal life. There had been no more Eddies. She couldn't help but wonder what her father might think about Michael Tolliver. New York was far from here. He was sophisticated and well educated, but seemed to be a genuinely decent man. This would go a long way with her father. Rene Arceneaux's opinion did matter, after she was still her Papa's girl. She thought about her sons and how a relationship might affect them. One step at a time, it had to go one step at a time. She glanced down at the bracelet lying on her desk. Putting it back into the tissue and then the box, she secured it in her desk drawer. The check went into the pile with Sunday's receipts.

Michael walked jauntily along the boulevard. He felt like a million dollars at least. After the dinner with Sally, he had spent a few hours in session with the group. Maybe his state of mind had affected his music, but it had been a superb evening. For the first time in a long time he started writing. A snatch of a melody worked its way into his head. This morning he began to put it down on paper. As soon as the stores opened for business, he rushed out to buy flowers first thing. The bracelet had been displayed in the window of the store next door to *Leoni's*, the flower shop. He hoped that it appealed to her taste. She was a woman that he wanted to *adore and adorn*. These were old fashioned, almost biblical words, but that was what he wanted, to adore her and adorn her. It was a monumental feeling. Her beauty deserved it. Her soul deserved it. She was another woman sacrificing herself on the altar of responsibility.

Hambone's friend said that she worked with Sally for almost three years and that during that time she never knew her to date or go to clubs or parties. Janette said that she was even surprised to see the Sally she knew, out of a white blouse and black skirt. He did notice that her clothing earlier in the day had been extremely simple. Again she had worn a blouse and skirt, but of a simple white fabric. Not a drop of cosmetic adorned her face. The wardrobe was obviously for her role at the restaurant. He still wondered about the café and how it had come about. But they both had things to learn about one another. Knowing that she worked so hard, he questioned what his next move might be. He needed to find a clear way to become firmly entrenched in her life. With her that meant finding a way to connect to her business. When it hit him, he couldn't believe that he had been so slow. He would play piano for her at her establishment. She couldn't turn down the gift of music.

10

A delivery truck pulled up to the front door of the café. Two large men efficiently offloaded their precious merchandise. No one was at the restaurant but the cleaning crew. Because it was deliberately scheduled for an hour or so before either Sally or Martin generally came in, the maintenance crew thought nothing of the other workers' movements. After all it must have been arranged. When the men rolled the gleaming ebony Baby Grand into the building, they barely noticed. Michael had given very specific instructions as to placement. Since he remembered the room's layout very clearly, the instrument was placed in a space nestled near the staircase. When the men drove away, Michael sat across the street. Driving away, he was very satisfied with the progress of his plan so far.

Sally came into the building late that day. Martin looked at her strangely, but she accounted it to his occasional oddities. When she walked into the main dining room, she felt that something was out of sorts. Until she put her foot on the first step of the stairs, it didn't dawn on her. Turning around without a pause, she went back to the desk at the entrance.

"Martin, where on earth did that piano come from?"

Now, Martin was totally confused. That same question sat on his own tongue from the moment that he arrived, but he'd restrained himself.

"Ma'am, I have no idea. You didn't order it?"

"No, of course not. What on earth would we do with a piano? There is some kind of mistake. It must have been meant for one of the clubs in the next block. Where is the invoice?" She looked around the desk.

"I haven't seen one, but the thing was here when I came in. The cleaning crew was leaving when I arrived."

"There must be some kind of paperwork or delivery information around."

The two of them went to examine the mysterious piano. Nothing was inside or attached. It appeared that a deliberate effort had been made to eliminate any clues as to its origin. Finally, after getting no answers from the kitchen staff, the pair gave up in frustration.

"Well, the mistake is bound to come out by tomorrow."

Sally was resigned to the presence of the piano for tonight. It was not possible to move it somewhere in the thirty minutes or so before the doors opened.

"Let's just throw some flowers on it and look silly if any of the patrons ask about it."

Sally went upstairs to dress for the evening. Martin did as she asked and placed one of the arrangements and a scarf on the instrument's gleaming surface. He had to acknowledge that it did add to the room's ambiance. While Martin was in the kitchen arranging a last minute detail, Michael slipped into the entrance. He thought that this must be how a naughty schoolboy must feel. Pranks were out of his realm of childhood experience, but not his imagination. He sat down and began to play.

Sally heard the first of the notes waft through the building as she finished dressing. Her first guess was that someone on the staff had not been able to resist the piano just sitting there. After a few moments, she decided that it had to be an early dinner patron. Oh well, she thought, at least it won't be wasted tonight. By the time that she walked down the stairs she had begun to enjoy the music. It was too bad that it didn't belong here, she concluded. At the sight of Michael sitting at the keyboard, she almost missed the next step and tripped. She stood for several minutes and watched him before slipping up close to him.

"What in the name of heaven are you doing?" Are you responsible for this piano being here? What were you thinking?"

The words tumbled out rapidly, but softly sibilant, in an almost hissing fashion. She did not wish to cause a scene, no matter how upset she was. Michael looked up at her and smiled pleasantly. He had expected something like this from her. He spoke as quietly as she did.

"God, you are beautiful right now! Good evening to you. What can I play for you?"

Sally's eyes were unbelieving. Someone must be playing some kind of a joke on her. This man could not have possibly had a piano sent here just to serenade and impress her. She forced herself to speak in very clipped tones.

"I am going to close my eyes and when I open them, this is not going to be real. You will not be here." All the time she knew it to be true.

Michael had never in his life enjoyed anything so richly as this. He smiled and continued to play. At that moment, a patron came over and congratulated Sally on the addition of the music. He made a request of Michael and walked away. As the music wafted across the room,

Sally stood there looking about her establishment. Without another word to him she turned and walked first to the kitchen. Later she passed him without a word and traipsed up the stairs. Michael continued to play for a couple of hours. Several people slipped bills underneath the shadow of the bowl of flowers. When he finished playing, he smilingly handed the money to Martin with instructions to divide it among the staff. As he started up the stairs, Sally opened the door to her office and stood there, expressionless. He swallowed quickly and walked in that direction. It was not easy to read her face. She hadn't come back down. He might have royally blown it.

"Mr. Tolliver, tell me. Would you like dinner? Were you playing for your supper? What the hell, exactly, are you doing?"

Her voice was calm, quiet and deadly. Michael was afraid now. Didn't she understand? He kept his tone light.

"Actually, I am famished. If you will allow it, I will be glad to play for my supper often." He decided that his best weapon was honesty.

Sally could not, for the life of her, figure this man out. Never in her life had she heard of anyone who… She looked at him. He sat there in the chair in formal dress, innocently, as though this was an everyday happening. But he was so appealing and down right good looking. Something about that dimpled smile created a melting feeling somewhere inside her, she realized. He was going to all this trouble just to gain her attention and favor. She looked away from him quickly. She was softening more and more. There was no question about it.

"I'll be right back."

She left him to his own devices while she made a quick run to the kitchen. Admittedly she was also hungry. When she walked back into the room, she carried a tray laden with good things. They said nothing of substance and ate like two small greedy children. Finally Michael patted at his mouth with the napkin and spoke.

"That was absolutely wonderful. I say I might have been overpaid for tonight's performance."

Now that he had broken the ice, she opened the drawer and took out the vellum box.

"Michael, I don't know what to think about you. However, I cannot accept this bracelet. It's more than a bit extravagant. The music was beautiful tonight…but, I…" She handed it to him.

"There's nothing I can do with it. I can't return it. Just discard it if you don't like it." He was very matter of fact in his response. He ignored her outstretched hand.

"I couldn't possibly throw it away. It's just that I don't know what it is that you want from me. The bracelet is beautiful, but too expensive. What are you looking for, from me?"

There were a few minutes of silence as he gathered his thoughts. His brown eyes looked into hers unwaveringly.

"Sally, I think that you are such a special woman. I believe that we could be good together. Please give it a chance."

He was sincere in his entreaty. By now he knew that he just wanted the opportunity to love her. The questions scared him, too.

Nothing was simple in this situation. Sally sat with the box in her hand. He was the best possibility that had touched her life in a long while, but she had to be honest.

"Michael, I am just a simple country girl. I have not traveled beyond the road that runs between here and St John Parish. My schooling was limited to what was available there. I have two children. Your life has been very different than mine in every way. I realize that men sometimes look at me and see only an object of desire, somebody to be used. How people see my looks is not my fault, because I am not willing to be that woman. I may not be perfect, but I will be nobody's whore. So if that's all you're looking for, get up and leave now."

Her huge doe shaped eyes were totally without guile. She had never been more serious in her life. Her lids lowered.

The dense ruffle of her eyelashes fluttered and lay on her cheek. She closed her eyes because she didn't want to see him leave.

Michael sat and listened to her impassioned statement. Here and now, he realized what he had failed to find in a woman before. All the women that he had been involved with had been so superficial. It would have been hard to make one real complete woman taking parts from each of them. Carefully, he leaned forward and placed a kiss on her eyelids. Startled, she opened her eyes wide and questioning.

"I am going nowhere. Sally, I don't know what lies ahead of us, but I believe that we have to explore our feelings. We are adults and I expect that our relationship will develop on an adult level. I will never, ever, disrespect you and I will always cherish you."

She looked at his face closely. It was a perfect man's face. His skin was a healthy coppery brown and just smooth enough. His eyes were clear with bright coffee brown centers. In the midst of his squared chin was a perfect cleft. She put a fingertip on his brow and traced each feature cautiously. It was as though she sought to memorize him, or perhaps to ascertain that he was indeed flesh and blood.

She stood up and took his hands, pulling him to his feet. Unsure what was happening, he made no other move.

When she wrapped her arms around his neck sinuously and kissed him deeply, he was almost shocked. The degree of passion was an immediate change from her reticent behavior of a few minutes before. It took every fiber of strength in his being to not lose all sense of decorum. His promises to himself, and to her, were going to be hard to keep if she kept this up. He returned her kiss with restraint. She put her head on his shoulder. He held her closely, thinking about the mere feeling of her. Sally's body sung in his arms. He remembered the empty embrace of the New York girl and chuckled. This was how a woman was supposed to feel.

"You feel good to me." He had to say it.

Sally noticed the same thing. Their bodies seemed perfect together. She had been so young with Bernard. This was a totally different feeling. It was also special and not the frantic thing that she had felt with Eddie.

"You feel good to me, too."

They stood for a few minutes longer, enjoying the comfort of each other's bodies. Sally was the first to move away.

"I need to see that everything is okay downstairs. How long can you stay?"

Michael didn't want to be presumptuous, but he wasn't sure what she was asking.

"How long do you want me to stay?" He tried not to sound too anxious. He was prepared to be patient with her, as patient as necessary.

"I will be back in a few minutes."

She was noncommittal in her reply and quickly walked out of the office. Michael felt like a kid again. Since he was unsure of her signals, he had to simply allow her the reins. He was prepared emotionally to venture into this relationship as quickly, or as slowly, as she chose. It was just that she was the most desirable woman he had ever met. He poured himself another cup of coffee to calm his nerves. After almost an hour, Sally returned to find Michael at the window, looking out at the nighttime scene. Her face broke out into a smile when she saw that he was still there. She rushed into his arms again. He held her as he had before. They stood together in front of the window. He determined that what they had together was certainly beyond passion. Even though he wanted so badly to make love to her, this would do for now, for as long as necessary.

Sally had performed the normal tasks and locked up downstairs. She kept pushing Michael to the back of her mind, but each time her eyes fell on the piano sitting in the middle of the floor. He had immense talent, of that she was sure. It had been such a joy listening to his elegant fingers trip across the keys. That kind of artistic skill fascinated her. What pleasure it must bring to be able to perform at that level. Envisioning his elegant fingers as they danced across the keyboard, she had to stop herself from substituting her body for the black and white pattern of the instrument. She thought that her spine might play similar notes if touched just so. Despite her speech, Sally knew that she desired Michael. All the things she said were true, but… She had needed to concentrate and focus to complete the tasks at hand.

"Where do you live?" She asked into his shoulder.

"On the edge of the Quarter, not far away. Why do you ask?" He was calculating how quickly they could be there.

"Oh, I just wondered. Do you live alone?" Her sultry voice was level and even.

"Of course. I am a bit too old to share lodgings if it isn't necessary. Would you like to see my house?" He held his breath and prayed. "It's only a few minutes by car."

"No, but perhaps sometimes soon. Would you play the piano, just for me this time?"

He took her hand and led her down the stairs. The room was dark except for the chandelier above the stairs. She lit the tapers of a candelabrum and placed it on the piano's surface. Michael had removed his tuxedo jacket. He wore a formal shirt with his trousers, and loosened the tie about his neck. She sat on the stair. Michael started out playing simple melodies and progressed to the syncopated rhythms of jazz.

Sally could not ever recall such a pleasure, simultaneously simple and acute. The music, the comfort of the circle of light and the intimacy combined to create an unforgettable experience. After awhile she walked over and blew out the candles. When she took his hand and led him back up the steps, he thought that they would say goodnight and simply exit the back staircase. Instead of turning toward the back stairwell, she led him into her office and through some French doors. There was an attached dressing room, or boudoir. He let her lead him.

In Sally's head the music continued. Making love to Michael was what her life needed. He was both a passionate and compassionate lover. Nothing in her past had prepared her for the depth of her responses. Michael discovered that he had been absolutely correct. She was a woman of substance. Making love to her was the equivalent of composing a symphony, well worth extraordinary effort. They found sacred solace in one another's arms until the first faint streaks of morning crossed the sky. He woke up to see her staring into his face.

"Good morning, my sweet love."

He spoke as he nuzzled the curve of her neck. Sally sighed with pleasure. This man had made her body do things that she never knew it was capable of. Whatever this relationship was, she wanted it.

"It's almost light, you should go." She hated to cast him out, but she needed to rush home herself. The boys would be up in a very short time.

"Is that why you asked how far away I lived?" He teased.

"Sort of." She said, giggling like a shamefaced child.

"So, you use me and toss me out."

He tousled her hair. That bobbed haircut was unbelievably cute on her. Everything about her was adorable. She had been an amazing surprise in bed. He kissed her and jumped from the bed. Sally watched him with pleasure as he strode into the office and came back with the bracelet in hand.

"Oh, I forgot to put it back in the drawer. Michael, you really should return it."

Sitting beside her on the bed, he took her hand and kissed it. Turning her arm upward, he kissed the inside of her wrist. Sally could feel her pulse beginning to quicken. Laughing, she tried to take back her hand.

"I don't think that you should do that, sir. I am a mother who has to depart this den of iniquity right now in order to tend to my flock."

Michael slipped the bracelet on her wrist with dexterity and leaned forward to kiss her mouth sensually, but quickly. Looking directly into her eyes, he did not smile and his words were delivered in a solemn tone.

"This bracelet is a symbol of the beginning of us. Wear it and be reminded of the sterling quality of the feelings that I have for you. Please accept it. Let me love you."

Somehow, Sally knew in her soul that everything about this man was real. She needed to love him, too. Holding her hands up, she simply held his face in her hands. In one shared look, a promise was sealed.

They took turns in the small bath attached, dressed quickly and left after tidying up the room. The cleaning crew didn't come into the office unless she asked, but to be sure she locked the door. Sooner or later, the staff would figure it all out. But for now, their love affair was her precious secret.

That morning the boys woke up to the smell of bacon frying. Antoine thought at first that he was dreaming. Because Sally worked so late and slept in, the two of them were accustomed to making their own grits or oatmeal in the mornings, then stopping in for a quick greeting before they left for school. Antoine stopped to consider the date. Was it somebody's birthday, or a holiday? He nudged his brother.

"Wake up, Bernard. Wake up quick!"

A sleepy Bernard glanced over at the clock to verify the time. He still had a couple of minutes before he had to get up.

"Man, leave me alone."

He caught the whiff of bacon coming from the kitchen. Suddenly, he too stirred and began to get dressed. His brother watched his change of attitude with amusement.

"I told you. Sally is in there cooking up a storm! I smell biscuits, too."

The two boys jostled one another through getting faces washed and teeth brushed. Within fifteen minutes they were dressed and walking into the kitchen. Sally sat at the table smiling, coffee cup in hand. Eggs, bacon, grits and biscuits awaited them.

"Good morning, darlings! I hope you're very hungry this morning." She was smiling and cheery.

The two boys looked at one another quizzically. It wasn't Christmas, or Easter. It was neither of their birthdays. This couldn't be their mother! They both answered muttering, "Morning." It came out sounding like "Moaning". Sally was suddenly conscious of everyone's accents. Being with Michael made her more aware of everything around her. From time to time she glanced down at her wrist and saw the exquisite strands of silver gleaming there, a promise that her life was perhaps, no longer unlucky.

The boys shoveled the tasty breakfast food down at record speed. They couldn't believe their good fortune. After cleaning the plates of seconds, they left for *St Theo's, the Catholic School for Colored Boys.* After the boys left the house, their mother decided that she truly needed some sleep, no matter how great she felt. She quickly drifted off into a dreamless sleep, touching the bracelet on her wrist.

Across town, Michael sat at his piano. His mind was not allowing him to rest. Sally had become a melody that would not leave his head. His fingers worked arduously to duplicate the sequences. He jotted notes to paper. Back and forth he went from keys to paper, until he was satisfied that he had captured the music that was trapped in his mind. She was everything that he had ever dreamed about in a woman. The differences that she detailed did not matter to him. Her heart, her spirit were what made her the woman he knew that he was beginning to love her without qualm. He admired her as a smart woman who handled her business well. Of course, the packaging did not hurt at all. He always prided himself on being the kind of man who did not chase skirts. He never lied to women to gain favor, or to access their beds. He had never found any real pleasure in empty adventure. Carrie's teachings had soaked in, he guessed. He truly believed in the sacred value of love. Sally's mojo had soaked into him even more quickly. He laughed, thinking about the voodoo myths that permeated New Orleans culture. He had come down here and been put under the spell of a Louisiana woman. Michael knew that Jeff would make that joke. He would just have to let him have his laugh.

When Sally walked into the café, she saw the piano and her legs went weak. The memory of the evening was still intensely fresh. A sensory memory flooded her system and she could smell the bay rum scent that he used as shaving lotion. Taking a few deep breaths, she steadied herself. There was a business to run. Her employees were still abuzz over the piano as well. Martin looked pointedly at it and looked at her. Sally had said nothing else about the instrument. No one had picked it up, so he supposed that it was staying. Truthfully, he did enjoy Tolliver's playing of the piano last evening, even though he didn't like his type.

Shortly after opening, Michael came in, sat down and started to play. His hands were a marvel. They were graceful, large and strong with long, tapered fingers. These fingers could literally dance across the keys. This routine went on for several days. After playing for a couple of hours, he'd have dinner. Sally looked forward to both his company and his music. The companionship was as sweet as the intimacy had been. He didn't push her to repeat the assignation. Each of them knew that it would be and that there was no hurry. Their emotional investment was long term. The diners responded well to the café's new feature. One after another, patrons made it a point to make favorable comments to Sally. A week or so had passed. On this evening, Michael came in as usual. This time he had Jeff with him. The diners were treated to a soft backdrop of the duo for two hours. At eight, they packed up. Michael came up the stairs and knocked. She opened the door with a kiss.

"Are you here for supper, Mr. Tolliver? The music was wonderful."

"No, I don't have time to eat, unfortunately. We have an engagement all week. But I will be here for a couple of hours beforehand. I have been thinking about something more permanent for you." He held her closely to enjoy her presence for a few moments at least.

"What are you talking about, Michael?" She didn't quite understand what he meant.

"It occurred to me that I could find someone to play here the entire evening for tips. There are some good people out there who are trying to get started… maybe a trio…"

She understood what he meant now. His music was actually his livelihood right now. He intended to give her whatever time he could. He had put the piano there, after all, but maybe she'd give him a little scare…

"Do you expect this trio to have meal privileges, too? What else do you expect me to dole out? Michael, what kind of a woman do you think that I am?" She stepped back and put one hand on her hip, pale eyes blazing.

Michael looked at her. 'Oh my God, did I say something wrong?' He thought. He ran his words back through his head. He grasped her shoulders in his large hands.

"Sally, what are you saying? In case you have forgotten my promise, I care about you deeply. I thought that if I could help give you a little leg up on the competition, it would be my contribution to your business's well being."

Suddenly, he heard the musical notes of her laughter and he realized that she was giving him a bad time. He shook his head, giving her credit.

"Okay, Miss Boss Lady, you win this one. I have to be off to the club date. I want to see you again whenever you will let me. I want to make that clear. But in the meantime, if it's okay with you, I will play here tomorrow." He kissed her on the forehead and taking her hand, the inside of her wrist, where the bracelet caressed her arm constantly as a reminder of his feelings.

"Go, go before I won't let you. We can talk about the other plans at another time."

On the way to the engagement, Michael was jovial and laughing much more than usual. When he started to whistle, Jeff spoke up.

"What the heck is going on? You are not the very cool guy that I used to know. Bring back my friend, please."

Michael looked at Jeff out of the corner of his eye. He did seem genuinely perturbed.

"Jeff, I think that I might have decided to settle here forever. I must be in love."

His friend became strangely silent. He exhaled in a long sigh.

"Michael, I would make a joke, but this is serious. You have seen this woman, what, once, twice?"

"No, we've been seeing one another for a couple of weeks steadily now, almost daily. Jeff, you know that I am not one to play around or to play games. I am also a good judge of character. She is an amazing woman."

Jeff Arnaud had never thought that he would be having this conversation with Michael, of all pcoplc. What was this woman about? He'd had to find out more than Hambone had been able to tell them. Michael Tolliver was a good guy and he deserved the best. At the back of his mind he questioned himself. Why did this affair upset him so? Shouldn't he be happy if his friend was so happy?

Sensing that Jeff had issues about his deepening involvement with Sally, Michael became quiet and thoughtful. He knew that sometimes friends didn't deal well with loss of a good friend to a love relationship. He would have to be careful not to be so damn happy. That was going to be hard! In fact, it might be impossible.

Michael found a younger group of musicians to provide permanent musical backdrop for the diners at Café Petite Rouge, three nights a week. They were competent, yet more than happy to play for tips. He sometimes sat in with them and sweetened the tip pot himself if he felt it necessary. At other times, the guys from his group would join him. With generous acknowledgement, Sally's patrons kept the group more than satisfied. The music had been such a rousing success that Sally fed most of them happily. Hambone, she laughingly complained, could eat her out of business. The bass player did have a healthy appetite, but his personality and talent more than compensated. The café's clientele had increased significantly. Two new staff members had been hired within a month of adding the music. Her business had always done well, but now it had moved to another level. Larger parties came in and lingered longer while spending indiscriminately.

The relationship with Michael was moving along nicely, Sally decided. Most interesting to her was his patient cultivation of their relationship. Whenever opportunity presented itself, they were intimate. Sally felt that they had discovered the formula for an ideal adult relationship. Socially, they were wonderfully compatible. His reverence toward lovemaking was the element she had unknowingly needed to create a heightened sense of existence. Her life felt perfect.

They had developed an easy pattern of dinners together. Conversation was unforced and easy. The staff became accustomed to his being there. He was courteous and pleasant to each of them and they responded in kind. Sally began to rely upon his presence. Often he insisted on helping her with her chores. It was interesting to him that without significant formal education, Sally was an astute businesswoman. Her instincts were excellent and her reasoning always sound. Michael knew that he had grown to love her deeply. The one thing that bothered him was her failure to include him in her home life. He appreciated the fact that they were having the opportunity to get to know one another well. But he really wanted to meet her sons. This would be the true test of the relationship. From time to time he managed to bring the subject of the two boys into the conversation. Sally readily answered his questions, but she seldom volunteered information. Initially Michael thought that she resented his intrusion into the other segment of her personal life. After several months he began to glean that it had nothing to do with him. She separated herself, too. The wall in Sally's life was as much for her own sake, as to keep anyone else out. He became even more intrigued. This woman was the person that he loved. He must find a way past her walls. His whole life depended upon it.

Antoine noticed that Sally was different most of the time now. It was nice that she didn't seem to be as tired. She smiled a lot, too. He remembered that when he was a little kid she was more like this. As time had passed, she had changed. When they were little kids she had some other job that didn't take so much time. He tried to talk to his brother about it, but Bernard never wanted to talk about Sally. Bernard was funny like that. He was kind of quiet and everything. One thing though, no one bothered Bernard, at school, or in the neighborhood. No one bothered him either, but because he was Bernard's little brother. He was one of those people who was good at everything. Bernard was tough, also really smart at school. The nuns were always picking on him because he wasn't as dedicated a student as Bernard. His brother was also always coming up with ideas to make money. He didn't care about that stuff the way that Bernard did. He wanted to do something special, but just didn't know what yet. Antoine was a dreamer. The nature of his dreams was yet to be determined.

The year had wound into fall. November had settled itself in with the heat abating itself somewhat. Days became as pleasant as the nights. Few trees changed color here and there was little difference in the weather. New Orleans had one real season, summer. Only the degree varied. Calendar summer was the major season and the fall season was summer minor. It was still warm and nights were slightly breezy. The beauty of southern nights was not touted highly enough. Michael had decided to walk the several blocks from his house to Sally's café. Tonight he had only the café and Sally on his schedule. He hoped that he would be able to convince her to have a shared holiday meal. It was two weeks until Thanksgiving and Sally had said nothing about celebrating the holiday together. It would be the ideal opportunity to meet the boys and, hopefully, her father. He had not discussed it with Sally, but he had actually seen the boys. His curiosity had finally gotten the best of him. One summer afternoon he drove over near her house. After visiting the corner store for a cool drink, he drove slowly down Orleans Street. Antoine and Bernard were tossing a ball back and forth in front of the house. They were big boys, bigger than he had imagined. Why didn't Sally show such handsome boys off? He suddenly realized that they were not like her at all. One of them bore her coloring, but they were unlike her otherwise. Seeing that they had to resemble their father, it made Michael uncomfortable to think that perhaps she did not wish to share them for that reason. Just maybe it was her method of holding onto the memory of her late husband.

Tonight Michael had a chance. As they had dinner, she talked about some additions to her menu. He often served as her sounding board. It was a good feeling to know that she did care about his opinion. When they had discussed the new dishes, he decided to be straightforward.

"Sally, before we know it Thanksgiving will be here. It would mean a great deal to me to spend that time with you."

She was quiet for a few moments. The calendar had not escaped her either. It was so difficult to take chances. Her life had been so perfect for the past few months. Yes, she had separated it into boxes. It had been comfortable, as well as simple, moving back and forth from box to box. She was afraid. There was no question that she loved Michael. Her heart sang when he was around. Never in her wildest dreams had she thought that a man like him would come along for her, even that such a man existed.

"Michael, I always want to be with you. But I have the boys to think of." She couldn't look directly at him.

Michael reached out and lifted her face up toward him.

"Sally, I love you. We are good together in every way. These months together have been the stuff of dreams. I want to marry you, better sooner than later. It's time to meet your sons."

She did not move. Her lack of response caused him to think for a second that he must have imagined his impassioned speech. She sat in the chair staring back at him. Her expression gave nothing away.

"Sally, do you love me?"

He worried that she might jump up and leave him here. She seemed skittish. In her mind, Sally wanted to scream, to laugh and cry. While she was controlling her surface reactions, her emotions were going wild. He really did love her! She had felt it, but she didn't trust her instincts. Somehow, it had never occurred to her that he would ask her to marry him. But she wasn't sure about the boys. What would happen? Would he like them, or they him? She had to take the chance.

"Michael Tolliver, don't you play with me. I love you. I never thought that I could love another man. You made a liar out of me. Do you know what you are saying? I have two half grown boys. Are you sure about this?"

He kissed her then. It was the softest, most gentle kiss ever. He had his answer.

They agreed to have the holiday dinner together. He asked that she allow him to meet the boys as soon as possible. Possible became that very weekend. Sally panicked on that Sunday morning. Her anxiety level was higher than she had ever anticipated. The plan was to spend the day at a neutral location. She thought that church and a picnic might work. He was game for whatever she proposed. She had told the boys that a dear friend would be picking them up for church and they would be spending the day together. Both boys responded pleasantly. After Sally left the room, her sons had exchanged knowing glances. When Michael drove up, they were excited. His shiny car was enough to gain the approval of the boys. Antoine was certain that he looked good riding away in that car. He kept punching Bernard in the side with his elbow. When they drove up to the church, that cute girl named Bernadette Wilson was looking straight at him. Antoine knew that the car made him special. Bernard, meanwhile, busily calculated in his head what something like this car cost. It was a little fancier than his mother's. He decided that he would have an even better one when he became an adult. Sally, meanwhile, worried what the boys were thinking. They seemed calm enough. Neither of them had asked any questions when Sally told them that her friend, Michael Tolliver, was going to spend the day with them. What Sally didn't know was that the boys had always wondered why their mother had no men friends. Sally was the prettiest single woman on the block. She was also one of the few who had not paraded a string of men past the neighborhood. Unbeknownst to their mother, Michael's appearance provided a sweet relief for her sons.

After church they drove out to a spot across the river. Sally felt that it was a more private place than the parks near Lake Pontchartrain. It was a nice chance to get some fresh air and get to know one another. Sally had packed a basket with enough fried chicken, potato salad and boiled crayfish to feed an army. For good measure, she included her prize pound cake. They located the perfect spot for their picnic and Sally set out the abundant array of food that she had packed. The fellows greeted each item with enthusiasm as she set out the feast. Sally's first thought was that she had certainly brought too much food. However, Michael and the boys were almost up to the task. It was the ideal ice breaker, though they were a bit shy with him at first. His abundance of natural charm and athletic prowess won them over easily. The two boys were clearly hungry for more male companionship.

Up to now, their grandfather had been the sole masculine influence in their lives. He came to pick them up as much as possible. This past summer, both boys had been in St John Parish for two whole months. It had been a wonderful change from the city streets. His place had enough room for them to roam about catching frogs, fish and the occasional snake. The old barn was the ideal clubhouse to spend the heat of midday. Rene often let them eat lunch stretched out on their stomachs in the old hayloft. Sally's dad had hated for them to leave since his life had space to fill also. The boys felt that they had no one else since Bernard's family had never been close.

A quick stop at home had allowed them all to change into comfortable clothes. Seeing her slip easily into a pair of overalls, Michael knew that she was not a pretentious woman. Before the afternoon was over, she was playing the tug of war game with the three guys. She and Bernard gave Michael and Antoine a rough time before collapsing into laughter. After the food was demolished, the two adults stretched out on quilts under a big tree that shaded them from the afternoon sun. The boys went closer to the water to explore. Michael had a surprise up his sleeve that required just enough of the hours left in the day. He got up and folded his quilt.

"Sally, are you awake?" He called out to her.

Lazily, she opened her eyes and smiled. It had been a perfect time in the perfect place. The verdant lacy shade of the grove of trees was one of the most beautiful spots in the area.

"Of course, what's up?"

"You are always claiming your country roots. I am officially putting you to the test." He held something behind him. The smile on his face was at least a million watts.

"Michael, what are you talking silly about? You can't get more country than where I grew up!"

He stuck out his hands. In them were fishing poles for all of them, as well as a bucket of worms. Sally could not believe her eyes.

"Please! What on earth could you possibly know about fishing, Mr. New York? Let's go!"

She jumped up from her place and they went off to find the boys. What Sally couldn't imagine was that Michael's grandmother took him fishing when the family that she worked for went to their cabin upstate. He always enjoyed the peaceful activity. Sally's father taught her to fish when she was a small child and she found it hard to believe that here was yet another thing that they had in common. The boys were delighted with this turn of events. Sunset found the dirty, tired and happy crew packed into the car heading back to the city. When they drove up to the door of the house on Orleans Street, they were already well on their way to becoming a family.

Sally walked into the café early on Monday. The sunshine had kissed her cheeks and nose. Her face was wreathed in smiles. Never had she been more beautiful. When Martin saw her, he stopped in his tracks. The slight sunburn was ever so flattering to her smiling face. Martin looked at her and instantly knew that the tall northerner had stolen her completely away. Even he had to be happy for her, reluctantly for them both. He could not help but wonder how it must feel like to be in love that way. Over the past several months he had seen that they were obviously pleasantly involved. His first inclination was to dismiss it as a passing flirtation, or an affair that would burn itself out in its intensity. He did know that Sally was circumspect about her life. This man was the first that he had seen her with in the several years that he had worked for her. On Saturday, he saw her getting ready for the outing. Everyone was bustling about her as she cooked the food herself that evening. Such degree of preparation must mean that she would include her family, so Martin took the initiative, volunteering to handle things at the café that day and the next if she didn't plan to come in. It had been easy enough to see that this was important to her. Now today, he could see that it had been successful. If Sally was happy, it could only help them all. It was not his usual nature to feel this way. He suddenly questioned himself. Why was he always so bitter? Maybe it was time for a change.

The atmosphere at the café sparkled. Observing Sally's happiness inspired her staff. The upcoming holiday season was already being anticipated. Thanksgiving was just the beginning. Christmas, New Year's and then, Mardis Gras, were to follow. New Orleans is a city that revels in its tradition and celebration. The people understand the value of having enough such pleasantries in life to try and balance the rough patches. Thanksgiving was just a week away. Sally considered closing the café completely for the holiday. Whenever she thought about the many people who relied upon establishments such as hers for any celebration at all, she also considered not wanting to deny her staff their own family atmosphere either. It dawned upon her to allow limited seating by reservation only. Only half of the tables would be for patrons. The remainder would be enough for the staff and their families, hers included. Hopefully, Michael would not object. She knew that it would be an adventure for her sons since they knew virtually nothing of her life away from them. That night when she told Michael of her idea, he enthusiastically encouraged her and asked if the musicians could be included. She absolutely agreed. When approached, her employees were excited about the idea. Most of them had assumed that they would be working anyway, so this plan assured that no one would have to be away from their families.

Weather and circumstances worked together to create a perfect day. The atmosphere was festive. Families showed up in force, dressed in their Sunday best. The boys had never quite grasped what their mother did for a living. Of course this was because Sally deliberately and successfully separated her life for all those years. When the two boys walked into the café and realized why Sally was away from them so much, they were extremely impressed. Bernard, especially, accorded his mother another level of interest.

Music played softly in the background throughout. As the afternoon wore on, for a period Michael took over the musical chores with Jeff and the group. When Antoine saw that Michael was a musician, he was fascinated. It had not occurred to him that someone as cool as Michael could also play music. He sat transfixed listening to the melodies of one of the finest groups around. The quintet had been approached about making records and the plan was in the works. A lot of the New Orleans jazz musicians had migrated up to Chicago, so the good ones that were left got a great deal of attention. Jeff's stellar reputation from his time in Europe had not hurt. Michael, Hambone and the others were solidly talented artists to complete the sound. This quintet had melded into an amazing musical force. Those who heard them knew it instantly.

That day, Sally had chosen to wear one of her signature dresses. It was constructed of layers of a sheer printed silk floral fabric with a handkerchief hemline. The pale gray background contained large cabbage roses in variegated shades from a rich ruby to a pale rosy pink. Swirls of metallic silver paint were brushed throughout the pattern, highlighted by the strands of silver hanging from her ears and encircling her wrist. Her high-heeled slippers were bright pink silk. Michael had never been more proud to love her. Being with her was akin to the possession of a precious jewel.

Before the desserts were served, several of the staff offered toasts. Sally was the subject of everyone's praise round the large table. When the employees finished, Michael stood and rang his glass with a spoon, asking for attention. Sally was somewhat surprised. She thought that he would perhaps thank the musicians, since she really had nothing to do with them. With everyone looking on, he dropped to one knee and proposed to her. Sally could only cry,

"You already asked me."

She was touched and embarrassed simultaneously. He took a small black velvet box from his pocket. Opening it, he revealed a diamond ring in an ornately engraved white gold setting.

"Yes, but you never answered me." He slipped the ring on her finger.

Sally Langlois knew that she was blessed. Her concerns were for her sons. She looked in their direction. Both of them were smiling and clapping wildly.

"I did, you just didn't hear me." She shook her head affirmatively. "Yes, Yes, Yes!"

"I don't believe in long engagements. How about a Christmas wedding?" He knew that this was the time and place to get the right answers.

"Yes, Michael… a Christmas wedding..." She turned to her staff. After a pause for the crowd to calm down, she said to them all, "You are invited to our wedding, here at Café Petite Rouge on Christmas Eve at six in the evening."

Her sons ran to her side and hugged her. Their one outing with Michael had won them over immediately and completely.

Jeff Arnaud watched the happy scene from a distance. His misgivings about Michael's love affair had not lessened. During the past few months he had said nothing more to Michael. When his friend failed to discuss the woman with him, he hoped that the relationship had toned down a notch. Unfortunately for him, he was the only one of the jazz quintet who had negative feelings about Sally. Hambone found himself feeling especially sentimental and leaned over to speak to Jeff.

"Ah, man. This is so romantic. It makes you believe again. Don't you agree, Frenchy?"

Jeff looked at him and almost snarled back.

"Believe in what? I believe that Michael is a fool?"

Hambone Williams cast a look at Jeff that should have withered his attitude.

"Please, you need to stop clowning around, Jeff."

"I am dead serious. The man should have availed himself of all this loose booty out here. He obviously didn't get around enough. She's just another high yellow country girl."

Hambone took Jeff by the arm and pulled him from the café. When they were out of earshot of the building, he took Jeff by the lapels.

"Jeff, I used to like you. I, once upon a time, even respected you. I have watched you get nastier and nastier. I don't like it. Michael was your friend first, but you are the one who is ragging on his happiness. He is one of the best guys I have ever met. What is your problem? That lady has never done anything to you!" He lifted the smaller man off his feet.

Color suffused Jeff's face. He was unbelievably angry at Hambone. What was his concern?

"Let me go! I have a right to my opinion! Why are you so worked up?"

"I am 'so worked up' because the whole crew is sick of your sniping remarks. I get to be the messenger. We want you to stop. Period. End of sentence… We ain't got time for the bullshit."

He thrust Jeff away from him. He started to walk back into the café and turned to say one thing more as Jeff stumbled to catch his balance.

"You need to stop and examine yourself. Jeff, you have always tried to be half ass slick. That was expected. You ran around trying to be the New Orleans answer to Douglas Fairbanks or somebody. I hear that you were the same way over in France. It's been okay that you were the star, because we admire and respect your talent. We ignored your getting over on women because they were generally women who put themselves out there for it. You ain't never before taken a disliking to someone like you have to Sally. Personally, I believe that you just might be jealous. When you all saw her for the first time that night, your mouth was hanging open just like his was. You need to remember that. Michael jumped out for the first time ever and went for the woman before you got a chance at her. I think it pissed you off."

He turned and went back inside.

Jeff stood in the dark street alone. He lit a cigarette and puffed away in the deepening chill of the evening. No one could have told him that Hambone, of all people, would call him out like that. They went way back. He and Hambone played together in the same group way before the war. He had been a real friend. When his father died and Jeff was overseas, Hambone wrote to tell him even before his anyone in his family did.

The big man had allowed Jeff to stay at his place when that Jamaican had come after him. Before he left for the war, Jeff had been involved with this pretty dark-skinned girl from near the Irish Channel area. This fine woman worked in a bar owned by this cool Jamaican guy. She was about five and a half feet tall and built… all curves and dimples. His nose was open for that woman. What Jeff didn't know was that she was the Jamaican's woman and when he found out, all hell broke loose. The man chased Jeff around town. One night he got close enough to shoot at Jeff in a club where he was playing. The entire group was on the low avoiding that crazy man and his big gun. He camped outside Jeff's house, so Jeff ended up climbing a fence in order to sneak away. Hambone allowed him to stay at his place for over a month. The fine brown girl finally convinced her boyfriend that he really was the one for her. Only when they were very cozy again, was Jeff finally safe. Hambone earned Jeff's eternal gratitude.

After a couple of cigarettes, Jeff came inside. As he approached the table, Hambone gave him a warning glance. He acknowledged his long time buddy with a nod. Walking over to Michael and Sally, he offered them his congratulations. Looking at the betrothed pair later in the evening, he knew that Hambone was so right. Michael Tolliver was an extremely lucky man.

Michael wrote his grandmother a long letter. In it he told her all about Sally and her sons. Most important of all, he explained that he and Sally shared the love that he had hoped for in his life. He sent her money to come to New Orleans for the wedding, as well as enough to purchase a festive new dress. Carrie Tolliver received the letter on December 5th. There was just enough time for the woman to make her preparations and board the train for the trip. Under no circumstances would the grandson that she devoted her life to, get married without her presence. Worry had clouded her mind for months. When Michael came home from France, she had thought that her worries were over. Surely now he would go ahead and get started with his life, so that fine college education could be put to use. When he didn't move on from New Orleans as he had originally planned, she was concerned. His letter had said that he was a musician. According to him, the quintet actually made a decent living playing music, even on some of those phonograph records. Carrie could not understand why he couldn't use that fine education to get a good job. Wasn't that why she sent him there, to that university in the first place? Now he had gone and got involved with some woman down there in Louisiana. And to make it worse, she was a woman with children! Carrie just didn't have a good feeling about it. She wanted to get down there as soon as possible and see for herself.

The plethora of plans for the wedding elevated the holiday season to an even more frantic pace. Sally felt that her feet didn't touch the ground these days. A slight chill had come into the December air. Working with Cora, Sally had made the decision about her wedding gown. She knew that she wanted something lovely with the feel of the traditional. Though it was not her first marriage, she wanted it to satisfy any of Michael's dreams for his wedding. Besides, her first nuptials had been nothing elegant, just a happy country gathering. She supposed that deep inside she expected to feed some of her own dreams also. Cora designed a creamy ivory dress that filled all of the requirements. The dress was made of heavy crepe de chine and was fitted down to the hip line. It flared into a soft trumpet style, ideally cut for Sally's curves. Over it she was to wear a hip length blouse of sheer ivory fabric embroidered with pearls and crystals. Cora had looked at pattern after pattern until she came up with the final design. Pearl ivory leather pumps with a Louis heel completed her Bridal ensemble. It was exactly what Sally wanted. As a final touch, Cora attached pearl and crystal sprays to a comb that was to be worn above her right ear.

No decorative detail was omitted for this special day, so the restaurant was to be almost as beautiful as the bride. Decorative sprays and bouquets were created for the staircase, doors and banisters. The two cousins were satisfied that every surface would be arrayed in an elegantly festive manner.

Michael and the boys had become fast friends. No one could have made him believe how smooth the transition would be. The three of them were as instantly attached as he and Sally had been. Emotionally, the three were probably imprinted identically. He, too, had been fatherless. When he and Sally took Bernard and Antoine to buy suits for the wedding, the tailor assumed that he was their father. Both the boys and Michael beamed proudly. It seemed that he was the missing part of their family puzzle.

Sally's dad had already come to town. He wanted to allow Sally and Michael as much time alone as they needed. For years he had prayed that his daughter would find a good man. After the successful meeting with her children, she quickly introduced Michael to her father. Even before the introduction, she was certain about her father's approval. After all, he had been the biggest proponent of her need for a new relationship. Her father saw Michael as just the kind of man his daughter needed. He had no question that his prayers had been answered. Unbeknownst to Sally, Michael had spoken to him privately shortly before the holiday. Renee had traveled down to New Orleans two days before and Michael had made a point to come over when Sally was at the café and the boys at school.

Opening the door, Rene was surprised to see his daughter's friend. He smiled and greeted him.

"Why, hello Michael. How nice to see you again. I'm afraid that you've missed Sally."

"No sir, I thought that perhaps I could spend a little time with just you this afternoon." He heartily shook the older man's hand.

"Fine, then come on back into the kitchen with me and have a cup of coffee."

Rene was impressed with the man that Sally was seeing. He led him back into the sunny yellow room and filled two large mugs. A few weeks before, Sally had brought this man out to meet her father. He knew then that the man was special to his daughter. Observing them, he had seen that something much greater than friendship existed between them.

As the two men settled themselves in Sally's cozy kitchen, Michael realized that he had spent little time here at this house, despite the depth of the relationship between them. He had picked up the boys to go fishing a couple of times and once he had come over for breakfast with the three of them. After exchanging general pleasantries, Michael spoke up.

"Sir, I know that Sally is your only child and I respect that relationship even though she is an adult. It is clear that the two of you are close."

"We are extremely close, Michael."

"I wanted to tell you that I love your daughter. She is the woman I want to make my life with. I will cherish her and care for her."

Rene looked closely at the tall young man sitting across from him. He appeared to be genuine.

"Does she know this? After all, Sally is not a girl, she is a woman with responsibilities and a mind of her own."

"Yes sir, I have made myself clear to her, but I am very aware that your opinion matters to her. I want you to know me and know my intentions. As for her responsibilities, I suppose that you refer to the boys."

"Well, I do. Not every man is willing to take on a ready made family. These children have needed a father. Are you willing to be their father, as well as Sally's husband? Sally is a beautiful, smart woman. Any man would want her, but she does have two sons."

"Mr. Arceneaux, nothing would make me happier than to be a father to those boys. They are a part of Sally and I love them just for that reason. However, I have gotten to know them and love them for themselves. I have a lot in common with Bernard and Antoine. You see, I grew up without a father, too. My father died when I was two years old, my mother a year later. My grandmother, who is a proud, strong and independent woman much like your daughter, raised me. So, those boys and I have much more in common than any of us could have known. But most importantly, I will love your family with every fiber of my being. I promise you."

Rene was more than impressed with this man. He had prayed for someone like him. But, like Sally, he had begun to believe that such a man didn't exist. He took a prolonged sip of the coffee.

"I have one more serious question for you, Michael Tolliver."

Michael felt like he was in the second most serious situation in his life. He had won Sally over and thought that she would marry him, but her father really needed to be his ally. Family was important to him. He squared his shoulders and looked the older man straight in the eyes.

"What is that, sir?"

"Son, you are from New York. Do you plan to steal my family and spirit them away north?" Rene's smile was the answer he needed.

"No sir, New Orleans is my home now."

The two rose and shook hands. Rene assured him that if Sally loved him, it was good enough for him. He patted Michael's back and embraced him. The pair of them sat for hours talking about everything in the world and nothing. When the boys came home, they were happy to find the two of them preparing supper together. It was an all male event, enjoyed by all. Rene had his opportunity to see the easy camaraderie that existed between Michael and his grandsons.

At Thanksgiving, he was just as delighted as the boys when the proposal occurred.

Six days before the wedding, Carrie Tolliver arrived in New Orleans. Michael drove to the train station alone to pick her up. Sally felt that she needed to allow the two of them some initial privacy. Hers was a wise decision. Michael's grandmother came with every intention of stopping the wedding. Her fears about the life that Michael had chosen were based on various half-truths and legends about Louisiana, and especially its women that she had gleaned over the years. When she stepped off of the train, she was unsure what to expect. Her second fear was that her grandson was leading some dissolute life style. Her ideas about *Jazz Musicians* were based on some fire and brimstone sermon that an itinerant preacher delivered about 'the devil's music' back in Georgia some forty years before. Instead of the bum she thought he might have become, a handsome, well-dressed man stood before her when she stepped off the train. He was the boy that she raised, but now matured. After collecting her luggage, Michael took her to the car. Carrie felt like royalty. This sleek, shiny black automobile was as nice as those that her employers drove. From the corner of her eye she examined her boy and saw that he appeared to be in perfect health.

Proudly, she saw that he had 'thickened up' some, so she knew that he was eating right. Inside, Carrie's misgivings were beginning to quiet. Maybe she was wrong about this Louisiana woman after all. But she must be some older woman who had pulled the wool over her baby boy's eyes. Why would he have gotten entangled with a woman with two children?

Michael asked his grandmother if she wished to freshen up before dinner. She assured him that the train had complete facilities and that she was fine. Her concern was getting to the heart of this thing. Just as Carrie Tolliver was running these thoughts through her mind, the car pulled up to Café Petite Rouge. In the winter twilight, the building created an exquisite picture. The Victorian architectural details made the perfect holiday scene even though New Orleans had no snow. Christmas wreaths adorned the doors and windows. The soft glow of the chandeliers cast a warm light onto the sidewalk. Christmas music, played by the trio, drifted into the night air. As the door opened, Sally stepped into the entry to welcome Carrie to her café. It was a picture perfect moment. Sally was resplendent in emerald green velvet, the perfect illustration for an elegant Christmas card. Michael thought that he could not have staged it better. The look on his grandmother's face as she entered the café was priceless. He had explained that Sally was the proprietor of her own business. Evidently Carrie had imagined something totally different. He was not sure which of the two was the greater surprise to his dear grandmother. She looked at Sally and him, then at the surroundings. By the time that they reached Sally's favorite dining room, Carrie Tolliver was virtually speechless. While she was no stranger to opulent surroundings, she was flabbergasted that this very lovely young Colored woman was the proprietor of such an impressive establishment. Sally had been prepared for some resistance from this woman, understanding what some of her objections might be and was determined to overcome them all. Sally had arranged for a dinner menu that Michael chose as his grandmother's favorites. Everyone in the café was focused upon Carrie's comfort and ease. The staff treated her like visiting royalty.

Carrie had worked hard for her entire life. Here for these moments, it was different. It was quite the experience. That evening she also saw that her Michael and this young woman loved one another. Her heart recognized the small signs as the true tale. They were considerate of one another. She observed the small courtesies and discreet displays of affection. Once she had a passion like this in her life, Michael's grandfather. Thomas Tolliver was a big strapping man who loved her with the same gusto that he embraced all of life. He laughed loudly, worked hard and perished in a sawmill accident before his thirty-sixth birthday. The owner had delivered a brown paper package containing his personal effects. It included a pair of overalls stiff with Thomas's blood. For years she kept that string tied package as a reminder of what she had lost.

Michael was beside himself with happiness. This was the first time that he had seen his grandmother in a few years. He knew that she missed him, but his quest for life had led him here. Sally was the love of his life and he was clear that his grandmother would not have made that choice for him. In his heart, he did know that Carrie was a fair, decent Christian woman and this would ultimately be the test. He was convinced that the older woman would see the same strength of character in Sally that he had seen. He could not pretend that her looks hadn't been the initial thing that had attracted him, but what had made him love her, was the person that she was inside.

Sally orchestrated the evening from one minute to the next. This was, without a doubt, the second most important event in her life. She would not leave it to chance. Every minute detail was planned. Martin Jiles had been lookout for the arrival of Michael's car. Her clothing had been tried and re-tried. The music playing was as she had requested. Three workers had scrubbed the exterior of the building and manicured the grounds to be absolutely certain that everything was spotless. With every element correct, she would leave the rest to fate.

Carrie was appropriately impressed. Through conversation she learned that the woman was widowed, like she had been. The husband had died in the same war that Michael had managed to survive. Wasn't a thing wrong with that, she had to admit. She listened when Sally talked about losing her mother, but finding Valerie Broussard. Miss Valerie's death especially touched her. Everything that the young woman said, she could identify with. She and those poor babies had been through so much. She had to give the girl credit. It had taken a lot of nerve for a young colored woman to go into a business like this. Another point that she had to acknowledge was that with her looks, Sally could have fallen into many a pit of iniquity. Before the evening was over, Carrie Tolliver was thankful that Michael had met such a woman. She had to admit that her looks were sort of flashy, but her Michael was a fine looking man and together, they were an astounding couple.

On the next day, Sally and her family hosted dinner at the house on Orleans Street for Carrie and Michael. The boys were well behaved beyond even the usual standard. Carrie and Sally's father got along famously since they were actually fairly close in age. Sally's parents had finally produced their one child when they were well into their thirties, while Carrie had given birth to her son when she was eighteen and Thomas was nineteen. At thirty-five, she became a grandmother, and a widow later that same year. Sally's father was one year younger than Carrie, who blushed as she noticed that he was a handsome and charming gentleman.

Christmas Eve was a slightly cool dry day, perfect for the wedding. Sally and Michael Tolliver were married as scheduled in a ceremony at dusk. Every corner of the café was filled with flowers and well-wishers. Everyone agreed that Sally was the most beautiful bride they had seen in years. Her father saw that she was indeed more strikingly lovely than she had been at eighteen. Sally herself thought that no man ever looked more dashing than Michael did.

Jeff, Hambone and the other members of the quintet were among the guests. They were now unanimous in wishing the best to the happy couple. Jeff had truly followed the advice given to him and examined his own motives. He began to look for more stability in his life. At this point he was a bit frustrated because there were not many women like Sally around.

The newlyweds allowed themselves a short honeymoon, so they spent a whole week alone, no café, no family. Locked up at Michael's house, they enjoyed just belonging together. Sally cajoled her new husband into playing the piano that occupied most of the front room of the house. For hours he performed solely for her. She was his most grateful audience, awarding him his applause in the confines of the bedroom. Sometimes while she slept, he labored over the keyboard. It was an idyllic time for the couple, but it passed entirely too swiftly.

11

They managed to transition smoothly back to their daily lives. The Orleans Street house actually had enough space to contain all of them happily. Since the boys shared a bedroom, there was a bedroom each for Rene and Carrie. Night after night, the newly combined family shared meals, laughter and love. Carrie's visit to New Orleans joyously extended through the New Year. The whole group spent New Year's Eve fishing across the river. Antoine and Bernard found themselves at the center of a real family. Now with grandparents and two parents, their lives had changed definitely for the better.

Antoine, especially, could not believe his luck. Michael had moved his piano into the house. What was once a cavernous and little used dining room, became a music room. Suddenly the home had a new, vibrant center. Michael saw the interest that the little boy exhibited in the instrument. He spoke to Sally about it one night as he was preparing for bed.

"Have you noticed that Antoine spends a lot of time messing around the piano bench?"

Already in bed, Sally sat up. More than once she had spoken to her youngest about that very thing. She did not want the boys to interfere with Michael's work.

"I am so sorry. I'll speak to him again." She was apologetic.

"No, sweetheart. That is not what I am trying to say. Excuse me for not making myself clear."

Michael touched her hand to assure her.

"I believe that he is interested in learning the instrument. If it is okay with you I would like to talk to him about it. We could set up a regular schedule of lessons. He plays around with some promise."

Sally shook her head, "Okay. If you want to be bothered..."

Her tone was doubtful.

Her husband reassured her, "Darling, as I said, I want to teach him. Believe it or not, I took lessons from the time I was about six. By high school, I earned money by giving lessons myself. It would be a good brush up for me. Besides, I believe that he needs something just his own. He seems to be in Bernard's shadow."

Inside her head, she thanked whatever made God send Michael into her café that night.

At some point soon, they decided, it was time to expand the business interests. He suggested that a private club would be a natural extension of the café. The quintet played many dates in local clubs operating under such guise. A combination of the both of worlds might be a good idea. Sally agreed, however she hesitated because of the questionable legality of what would basically be a speakeasy. After considering the idea, she consulted Andre Fouchet because she trusted his counsel. The attorney gave her information regarding all aspects of the laws involved. He, too, saw the opportunities in the *laissez faire* atmosphere of a city such as New Orleans. The key, he agreed, would be in the airtight legal structure of such a business. As he provided sound advice and assistance for fair fees in the past, Andre Fouchet did again. Under the corporate framework that he devised, the Tollivers opened the private supper club. Simply stated, patrons paid an membership fee and a nominal sum for monthly maintenance. The rolls would be strictly kept.

As the couple scouted locations, it suddenly dawned upon them that Michael's house was in the ideal location. It sat on a corner lot fairly close to the café. Also, it was in an area near the French Quarter appropriately zoned with a commercial option. As fate would have it, Michael had held onto the property with vague plans to rent it out. When they noticed that the house next to it was vacant, the plan was sealed. By acquiring this house and one more, the space was sufficient. Entertainment would provide a primary feature of this new establishment. Michael negotiated appearance contracts with the members of the quintet and they agreed to regular engagements over a period on an exclusive contract. Any New Orleans appearances would be here. Vocalists would be hired in the same manner. The stability of such contracts was attractive to the artists. Music would become as steady as any other form of employment.

An astute head for business and a tight rein on purse strings had made Sally a wealthy woman. Marriage was not going to change her. She kept Michael focused and targeted. His first inclination had been to upgrade their personal lifestyle. His wish to give Sally the world, had to be held in check. She had to temper his extravagances on her behalf. Just as this thought crossed her mind, Michael came bouncing into her office with a huge silver package tied in red ribbons. A smile as wide as the Mississippi River graced his handsome face. Holding out the package, he could barely contain himself. The words came tumbling out.

"Hello Mrs. Tolliver, you know that you are the love of my life. You do know that, right?"

"Michael, what on earth?" Sally could not imagine what might be in such a large box.

"Open it, just open it. As I came onto Canal Street, this called your name from the shop window."

Sally immediately knew that she would most certainly have a problem. He would not understand that she had more than sufficient clothing to cover her needs. When she needed something, she went to Cora.

"Michael, you know that Cora provides all my wardrobe needs. She can..." he put his finger to her lips.

"Cora can not provide every single thing that you deserve. I repeat..."

At times he was difficult to reason with. Sally sometimes allowed Michael to do things for her that she would never have done for herself. Her patience was occasionally tested.

"But Michael, you know that we have the club opening coming up. I was just reviewing the expenses."

"Yes and so did I. The budget is on target. Besides, this money is found money. Jeff repaid me an old debt. Remember the club date last year when the guy stiffed us? He came through finally!"

Sally had never believed that story. She knew the man to be a sound businessman. But her questions about Jeff were another story. Something was not quite right. Michael seemed to be turning a blind eye when it came to his old friend's stability.

"Oh, I see. But Michael honey, just because it was an old debt that does not mean that the money should be squandered."

Michael was becoming impatient. He did not expect to be lectured. The expression on his face started to change. Sally caught herself. She kissed him and accepted the large box. As she opened the ornately wrapped package, she supposed that it was perhaps a new evening gown. At least she could use it for the opening next month. When she removed the paper, she saw the store's name on top of the box. Never in her life had she even been inside ***Jacobitz's***, a pricey Canal Street salon that was the shopping haunt of New Orleans' wealthiest people. She had heard that the family who owned it were nice people, but… As she opened the tissue to reveal the box's contents, she thought she would faint. Inside were layers of sumptuous fur, a full-length blue fox coat. Its variegated tones were the perfect complement to her smoky gray eyes. Various shades of gray were mingled to create an elegantly diverse color.

"Oh, my God! Michael! Have you lost your mind?" She ran her fingers through the thick soft fur. The silvery colored silk lining was as luxurious as the exterior of the obviously expensive coat. Inside, the store's signature label and her initials were exquisitely embroidered in red silk thread. As she stroked the fur, she caught Michael's expression out of the corner of her eye. His beaming smile clearly said that his pleasure was even greater than hers.

As she withdrew the lavish length of fur completely from the box, he held it and assisted her. Never in her life had she thought that she would own such an item of clothing. Sliding into the silken lined garment, she luxuriated in the feel of it.

"Michael, I can't keep this. It is just not practical down here in the heat. How often would I wear something like this? Let's be realistic."

"I can think of many practical reasons why you need it. First of all, happy birthday!"

She hadn't ever mentioned her birthday to him. She seldom thought of it herself. Today was August 17th.

"But, how did you know? I sometimes forget myself."

"Sally Tolliver, it's on the Marriage License. Remember?"

"Okay, okay. Michael, I love you so for wanting to give me such a wonderful gift. But we live in New Orleans. I would not get to use this magnificent coat as much as it deserves. It is just not a reasonable thing to do."

He continued to smile. From his breast pocket, he withdrew an envelope. He put it in her hand. Feeling breathless, Sally was almost afraid to open it.

"What is this? Michael, what in heaven's name is this?"

"It is the explanation, the answer to your questions."

Her hands began to tremble. Inside the large envelope were tickets for the train and some hotel information.

"New York! Michael, we couldn't possibly," She couldn't complete the thought, let alone the words.

"Yes, we can and we will."

Michael had planned this trip since the wedding, actually, before. He wanted to show his city to her and the boys and vice versa, he wished to show off his family. But he had not been totally honest with her about the money. Yes, Jeff had given him money owed to him. But it had been a great deal more than his share of a club date. Jeff had borrowed money from him numerous times. Using his personal funds, he never mentioned it to Sally. Jeff was still his oldest friend and right now he worried about his stability. Sally brought him out of his disquieting thoughts.

"Michael, with the opening next month how could we possibly leave town as soon as Christmas?"

"Sweetheart, I have it all figured out. Marty can handle the café. No question, right? Hambone has stepped up. We can have guest artists to fill in. He can handle the club and we both know that it will work."

Sally thought about it for a moment. Truthfully, Hambone had taken over booking talent for both establishments. He and Michael were managing several groups now. Since he had married Janette at the first of the year, he was a new man. Sally had been surprised to see Janette last Thanksgiving. She could not believe that after working with her for three years, the two of them ended up with husbands who knew one another. Recently she had been talking to her about coming to work at the café. With the new business, her time was beginning to be pinched. Janette could be a big help to Martin, especially since it turned out that Martin knew Janette from growing up in the same neighborhood. According to Hambone, she and her sister had been among the few people that Martin Jiles chose to speak to around there. Sally thought that Martin might have had some interest in the younger sister, whom she noticed, never failed to get a smile out of him during Thanksgiving dinner. She was hopeful for him. The man needed a life.

Everything was falling nicely into place, Antoine looked forward to the piano lessons twice a week. Already he had learned the keys and some basic melody patterns. His second favorite thing to do was to just listen when the group came over to practice. One day he wanted to play like they did. Maybe he could learn more than one instrument. Sometimes a guy sat in with them on another kind of keyboard called a xylophone. It seemed like a cross between a piano and a drum because it was played with something like padded drumsticks. The sound of it was really interesting. Hambone's bass looked cool to play, too.

Antoine thought that he would like to learn to play every kind of music that there was.

Bernard was not at all interested in music. He was, however, fascinated with the money that was made. Whenever he heard anyone discussing details of bookings and contracts, he paid close attention. It seemed to him that entertainers were well paid for doing something that was basically fun to them. It was hard for him to believe that the group considered what they did as work. Knowing Antoine, he wanted to learn music because it was another way to have fun. None of them seemed to understand how serious life was, so Bernard thought.

Sally now allowed her older son to help her make supply lists sometimes. He ran errands, taking her orders to the grocery supply house that was located nearby. The men would deliver the food and goods the next day. Dutifully, he would check the lists against the actual delivery. It gave him something special to do when Antoine had piano lessons. She wondered why she had never noticed how like a little old man he was. He and Antoine were opposites in personality. None of the neighborhood boys bothered Bernard. He was subject to sock anyone who made the mistake of teasing either him or his brother. The toughness was so unexpected in a smart kid like Bernard. Sometimes he scared his mother a little. Both boys were happy with their new life. It was like they had their mother back in a way they'd never had her before. They appreciated Michael for making them a real family. His solidity appealed to Bernard as much as his artistic side appealed to Antoine. It was as though all of them were supposed to be together.

Michael had stopped gambling at the after hours joints shortly after he and Sally became involved. His instinct for cards had been excellent, but he refused to take chances with their future. He did, however, begin trading on the stock market. The attraction of the Bull Market was impossible to ignore. He invested several thousand dollars in one of the new corporations that employed several of his former college chums in New York. International Business Machines was being touted as revolutionary. Michael dismissed the thought that the company was going to do all that was being whispered, but a solid return was all that he sought. Another investment that had attracted him was an airplane company. He had seen what some of the planes had done in the war and was quite impressed with the ideas of commercial application. Even more fascinating was the proposed development of larger planes to carry hundreds of passengers. Michael sought to create a solid financial base for his family's future. Economics had been a favorite subject during college and he sought to apply what he had learned to life. Seldom did he discuss these business ventures with Sally because more than once she dismissed the ideas as 'pie in the sky'. She was a firm proponent of the service philosophy that in order to make money, a service or product must be provided. Each of them quietly advanced their fortune by adhering to their personal beliefs about money.

Thankfully, they shared the basics. Among the basics, the supper club acquired a large subscription for membership. This assured that the venture would be profitable. Because Prohibition still held the country in its grip, certain arrangements were necessarily made. Alcohol was procured through intermediaries. Legally, the club patrons were responsible for procuring their own liquor, but in reality it would be a speakeasy, illegally serving alcohol. The proper palms had been well greased to avoid the stigma facing interference from police and legal entities. Sally was nervous about this part of the business, but her attorney had helped them to handle every loose end. No problems were encountered. Michael was in charge of the dealings with those suppliers who transported the alcoholic wares. Michael's eastern roots helped them to relate to him since many of these men had also transplanted from the east coast. Sally knew that these were dangerous men, despite the well-tailored suits.

The opening of the club was a phenomenal success. Nothing like *The Private Reserve* had been seen in these parts. The elegant atmosphere rivaled the best seen in Manhattan and Chicago. Socialites freely rubbed shoulders with local entertainers and any others who could afford the sum of the subscription. It was the place to be seen. Unlike the café, this atmosphere was anything but traditional. Trendy art deco style had been utilized in decorating the interior. Mirrors and sleek modern lines dominated. Sally caused a major stir in the silver chemise and matching cloche she wore on opening night. Cora had created the figure skimming dress and hat from a fabric covered in mirrored paillets that shimmered like a million stars. Because the weather had become unseasonably cold, she wore the amazing blue fox coat. Every eye was on Sally Tolliver that night.

Among the newly subscribed members of the club was a man named Enrico Barone, a wealthy forty year old who had moved from New York two years earlier. An avowed jazz patron, he had followed the quintet since they had begun picking up odd club dates. *The Reserve* served his tastes in every way, attracting him as one of its initial subscribers. On the night of the opening, he attended with his wife and a table full of guests, friends who were also wealthy and equally powerful. When Sally and Michael entered the club that night, all eyes went to them. Enrico Barone saw Sally for the first time and was entranced.

He had heard stories that the entrepreneurial musician's wife was a stunning woman, but this was his first sight of her. As the night wore on, Michael and Sally circulated among the guests thanking them for their patronage and encouraging their return. A constant buzz surrounded them throughout the evening as the patrons observed that the owners were an equally attractive, sophisticated couple. Barone was almost speechless. Though he had seen many attractive women in this city renowned for them, Sally was unusually tall and regal. His eyes devoured every inch of her. As the evening wore on, he became irritated with his wife and left much earlier than originally planned. Visions of the long legged woman in the short, mirrored dress would not leave his mind. He did not think of her as colored, her skin was hardly different than that of his wife Carla, a lovely petite woman of Sicilian heritage. She couldn't quite figure out what was wrong with Enrico tonight, after all that nightspot had been a lot of fun. While her husband was a man of mercurial temperament, his behavior was more unusual than ever before. As she readied herself for bed that evening, she noticed that he was lingering in the shower longer than usual and wondered what could be on his mind. His business interests often caused him to be less than pleasant, but she had learned to live with his mood swings.

12

After the splash of the grand opening, Sally did not make it a point to frequent *The Reserve* since her duties were primarily behind the scenes for that business. The dual operations required a great deal more administrative effort on her part. At any rate, she was not totally comfortable with the freewheeling club atmosphere. Unless the occasion required it, she preferred to allow that venue to remain Michael's primary responsibility. Her life was busy enough these days since the opening of the club had bolstered the café's business. Most nights she had all three private dining rooms reserved. It was as though the Tollivers were at the center of a segment of New Orleans' social universe. A diverse, wealthy and talented group of people circulated through the couple's business entities. Members of the club made it a point to frequent the café and vice versa, both businesses were booming. Sally often felt slightly fearful because it seemed that their lives were golden at this moment. Michael was the answer to all that she ever could have dreamed of in her adult life. Her husband, in turn, felt himself to be blessed. Not only had he found a woman beyond his dreams, but he was happily occupied with his widening business interests. A couple of the local groups, which he now represented, were in demand as far away as Chicago and New York. The upcoming trip could be used to make some additional contacts and transact business in person. Arrangements were made to have telephone lines installed in both businesses in order to facilitate his activities. All plans were in place for the family's holiday journey. Both Sally and Michael's staffs were clearly prepared to handle any eventuality.

The several months had passed by quickly. It was now December and the four of them became more excited by the moment. Wardrobes had been assembled. Luggage was purchased and packed, awaiting the departure. Both adults kept themselves at a lower key in an attempt to contain the level of excitement that both boys were exhibiting. Generally, Antoine displayed more emotion in any situation. Bernard's curious mind got the best of him this time and he was the family member most excited about going to New York. He read books and asked Michael question after question about every aspect of traveling and about New York City itself. By the time of departure, he was the family expert on all things New York. Sally realized that the cohesive success of her new family was most clearly illustrated in the respect and affection she saw in Bernard's eyes. He was no longer that overly reserved miniature adult. Michael's true measure as a man was reflected daily in the eyes of her two sons. Her constant prayer was that she not ever have to wake up from the dream that her life had become.

Boarding the train was a great adventure for the boys. Aside from the short car trips to visit their grandfather, like their mother, they had never left New Orleans. Sally felt the same level of excitement inside. Despite all of the preparations, her concern was that she might have missed some vital item. While she was eager to see the fabled northern city, her concerns were that she and the boys present themselves in such a manner to make Michael proud. They were, after all, going to visit his home.

The train journey was interesting, but uneventful. Bernard kept them informed of the geography as they traveled. The Pullman car porters were extremely solicitous of the young family. Michael understood that the key to a successful trip lay with obtaining the goodwill of the train's staff. He had generously tipped the men as they boarded the train. These men made sure that the handsome colored family did not suffer any undue indignities. While these men would most probably have treated his family extremely well under normal circumstances, Michael's gratuity assured this. He understood survival in the world around him. His dignity and self-assurance earned him the notice of these men, while his treatment of them earned him their respect.

Along the way a few acquaintances were made and the boys joyfully observed the varied countryside as the train chugged its way north. Nothing in their short lives could begin to equal this experience. Coming through Mississippi, three children waved happily to them from the back of a mule. Back home, a mule pulled the ragman's colorful cart, but never had they seen anyone ride on its back. Antoine loved to see the large wagon come around the neighborhood. From blocks away, he could hear the voice of the ragman raised in his singsong plea, "Rags, rags! Any rags today?" Strung along the canopy of the wagon's covering, brightly colored bits of various patterned fabrics flapped in the breeze like the flags of a long lost member of a gypsy caravan. Observing the mule, it had never occurred to Antoine that the odd creatures could be ridden. But here were these three boys crowded together carrying fishing gear and large circular metal syrup cans. Waving to them one last time, Antoine wondered if they were impressed because he was on a train. As they rolled along the tracks through state after state, the red clay and dense woods of the south gave way to a gentler landscape. The simple architecture of the eastern coastal towns looked more like pictures than real life. Bernard noticed that these towns were orderly looking and he wondered if that meant that the people were more serious than those back at home. He might like the north. Finally, the announcement was made for the arrival into New York City. When they departed the train, fluffy poufs of snow were falling. As the flakes of soft brightness aimlessly drifted past the multitude of lights around them, Antoine was amazed. Never in his short life had he seen snow. As he held his face up to feel the softness of the flakes he noticed that everywhere, buildings pointed up to the heavens. In New Orleans, only a few buildings even approached these heights. He seldom got a chance to go down to Canal Street to ever see those. This New York was some place special. He bumped into his brother as he turned to look this way and that. Bernard was trying to act so cool, Antoine thought. He knew that his brother was just as excited as he was. In the melee about them, the boys observed all kinds of people pushing and shoving. Each of them was in such a hurry, reminding Antoine of something. Then he remembered the metronome, the funny clock-like thing that Michael set on the piano when he did his keyboard exercises. These thousands of people all seemed to move around to the rhythm of thousands of timers. Everybody rushed to the sound of tick, tick, as though they were afraid to miss a beat. Antoine laughed aloud at his vision. He felt the pressure of Michael's hand on his shoulder as he steered the family into a taxi.

The hotel sat at the edge of a vibrant colored community that Michael told them was called Harlem. He explained that many gifted artists, writers and musicians lived here at this time. Bernard viewed the myriad of well-dressed colored people about him. He was accustomed to seeing the gathering of people at church where everyone always looked nice, but this was different. He couldn't quite put his finger on it, but this place had a good feeling to it. He just might want to live in New York when he grew up. Michael had told him lots of things about the city of his youth. Bernard liked the purposeful look of it all.

Carrie spotted her family when they arrived at the desk in the lobby. She had sat patiently for over an hour. Michael told her that they would come to her after they were settled. She couldn't contain herself. Waiting that long was out of the question. Looking at the four of them from a distance, no one would know that they were not a blood family. The boys had certainly grown. She loved just seeing Michael and Sally together. Anyone could feel the love there. Besides, it made her so proud to see them out in the world and know that they belonged to her. They were a beautiful and prosperous family, her family. Here in New York some people were really feeling the pinch from that stock market crash. Her people were not affected, but this was not true throughout her employer's circle of friends. One of the judge's cronies had blown his brains out, while another had jumped from a skyscraper. Oh well, as she had always told herself, it was best not to dwell on the bad things. She gingerly raised herself from the big comfortable chair and went to greet her family. The boys saw her first.

"Grandma Carrie!"

They ran to her. She so appreciated having more people to love. The time that she had spent with them had been wonderful. Since then a stream of letters had gone between New York and New Orleans. Michael kept trying to talk her into moving down there. So many years had passed since she had left the warm climate in Georgia. New York winters took their toll on her these days. It was true that the heat might feel good to her arthritic bones. She was still thinking about it. Gathering the big boys into the circle of her arms, she smothered them with kisses.

"Hello, my loves. Grandma Carrie got your letters and Santa Claus told me that he would change your address for this Christmas delivery."

The boys looked at one another. Did she think that they still believed in Santa Claus? Well, they would humor her.

"Yes, ma'am." They spoke in unison. No need to upset her, she was kind of old.

By this time Sally and Michael had walked over to join them. When all the hugs had been exchanged, the happy group went in to dinner. Over a marvelous meal they caught up on personal news. In the midst of the chatter, Sally took notice of the details in the big city restaurant. Her mind began to form an idea. After all, she had started out in a hotel restaurant. The possibility of a hotel intrigued her. Not one of the hotels that catered to colored in New Orleans was as grand as this one. In fact, they were a sad excuse if the truth be told. Sally's business head started functioning in high gear. She thought about the many entertainers who traveled back and forth. There were many colored who came to the city as tourists, as well. Mardis Gras was the city's grand event for all colors, all possible hotel patrons. In fact, the availability of a topnotch hotel could greatly encourage colored travelers. A small topnotch hotel might be the ideal next business step. Filing the idea away to speak to Michael later, she brought herself back into the here and now.

Michael had removed the rakish black fedora that he wore and placed it atop his fine wool coat. He looked about for the headwaiter and motioned him over. The man acknowledged him and approached the table.

"Are you ready to order, sir?" he was polite and friendly. Michael looked up at the man. A question entered into his eyes.

"Dickson?" He asked.

"Yes, I am Matthew Dickson." The man looked carefully at Michael. Then he recognized him.

"Sir, how good to see you. It's been a long time." After holding out his hand to Michael, the waiter turned to the ladies.

"The Captain here saved my life. He was a fine officer."

Carrie beamed with pride. Michael had never talked much about his time in the war.

"Sir, I haven't seen you here before. Aren't you a New Yorker? I never had a chance to properly thank you since I was shipped out from the unit, then to a hospital. Then after the war I came home to Harlem and always regretted that I had never gotten the opportunity to say how much I appreciated what you had done for me."

Michael explained that he now lived in New Orleans with his family. When he introduced her and the boys as his wife and sons, Sally fought back the tears. The man complimented his former officer on his fine looking family and Michael was sincerely proud. His hero status jumped one more notch with his family.

Matt Dickson was honestly pleased to see the captain looking so prosperous. Unlike a couple of the other colored officers, Michael Tolliver never treated his men poorly. He commanded them with respect and never bullied anyone. Matt always felt that some of the officers tried to forget the shabby treatment that they themselves received at the hands of the white officers, by mistreating their own men. One thing about Captain Tolliver, Dickson thought, he was the real thing. No one ever heard anything about anyone of either color trying to mistreat him. He still carried himself with that same dignity. Dickson chuckled to himself. He remembered that the Captain was also never known to chase after those foreign women. With a fine looking woman like that waiting on him, he thought, why would he? It was so good to see his old Captain. Of course, Matthew Dickson had no way of knowing that Sally was only a part of Michael's post war life. In front of him, he saw a cohesive family unit, one that any man would be proud of. His influence would be extended to be sure that they received all around top-notch service while they were here.

After dinner, Michael saw Sally and the boys to their suite of rooms. When they were settled in, he took Carrie home in a taxi. This way they were able to spend at least some private time together. She fixed coffee for him and they spent time mostly discussing Sally and the boys. Carrie could not help but think how she almost made the mistake of opposing his marriage. Who could have thought how well it would turn out? She looked at her baby boy sitting there in her neat suite of rooms. Michael was the picture of his grandfather Thomas, big, handsome and sweet as could be. But her grandson had that added quality which education and money brought, she observed and it made her proud to bursting. After promising to her God that she would see to it that her grandson had a better life, she had given him the tools to create it. Her job was done. Maybe she could rest a little herself. Maybe next year she would go down there like they were always asking.

During the New York visit, everything went by in a whirlwind. Michael found that he was in a rather enviable financial position right now. He was able to further increase and stabilize his portfolio with a few stocks that he was able to pick up at bargain rates. Meanwhile, Sally had even less faith in trading, having witnessed first hand some of the tragic after effects of the crash. Afterwards, she had approached him carefully. Had they been affected? Though she did not wish to admonish him, she needed to know. Her own nest egg was solid and she had made adjustments to be sure that the business entity remained clearly viable. Michael had always been on the cusp as an investor, avoiding any sizeable losses. His assurance that they were fiscally solvent in all regard relieved his wife immensely. In addition, his burgeoning entertainment empire was beginning to take on a life of its own.

While in his hometown, Michael was able to make a few contacts, booking a couple of the groups into quality locations. He knew that his interests still needed a trip to Chicago. Thoughts of leaving his family for that length of time did not appeal to him. He would have to make some kind of arrangements. Sally decided that she loved New York, but only to visit. The biting cold was not her favorite type of weather for any extended period. However, it was fun to wear her fox coat and not feel silly. Michael had bought her a matching fur cloche as an early Christmas gift. She knew that the ensemble was flattering to her. Not only could she see her reflection in mirrors, but in the eyes of other women. When other women look at you admiringly, she felt that you could be sure that your appearance was right.

She had such an experience when they attended church with Carrie. Michael attended this church growing up and obviously knew many of the people there. Sally was particularly aware of a woman who stared at her throughout the service. After Benediction, the woman pushed her way through the throng of people who sought to speak to them. An attractive woman of their age range with her black hair pulled tightly back into a huge bun, she pushed her way to them. Sally remembered that in the city the hairdo was called a chignon and noted that she wore it well. When the woman touched Michael's arm in a certain manner, Sally knew. There was something proprietary in the way that the strange woman put her fingers on the sleeve of his coat. Sally looked carefully at her. Of average height, she saw that the woman did have a very trim figure. Almost as fair as Sally herself, she wore bright red lip rouge instead of a more flattering rose shade. Though this had the effect of making the young woman look stylized and somewhat unnatural, Sally noted that her features were rather pretty.

As the woman pressed closer to Michael, she smiled broadly and directly at him.

"Hello there. It has been years since we have seen you in these parts."

Michael turned to Sally immediately and put his arm about her shoulders before he replied. "Francie! How nice to see you! This is my family, my wife Sally and my sons, Bernard and Antoine. Sally, this is Francie King, whom my grandmother once had hopes that I would marry."

Carrie moved forward at that moment. She interjected quickly. "Francie, how nice to see you. It sure is a good thing that Michael knew his own mind. He couldn't have a more perfect family."

The woman had a somewhat confused look on her face. Both Michael and his grandmother had dismissed her in some subtle way. She looked up at Sally, whom she could finally see clearly. In her eyes, Sally saw her thoughts reflected.

"It's nice to meet you, Francie. I surely do appreciate knowing that Michael was in such capable hands before mine."

The syrupy southern tones were disarming to all. Clearly, Michael's beautiful wife was no pushover. From behind them came a sudden intake of breath. Sally thought for a moment that she had been a bit harsh. The voice behind them then broke into a chuckle. Francie King was beside herself. She could not believe that they had treated her so shabbily. Turning on her heels, she quickly exited the building.

Later that night when they were alone, Michael told Sally about his relationship with Francie. She had been a sweet girl with whom he had kept company while both were in their late teens. As they got older, he realized that she had no substance. He told his wife how Francie had literally seemed to feel empty and lifeless when he put his arms around her. If his memory served him, he said, her clingy displays of passion had seemed artificial. Sally put out her arms to him.

"Come here." She said.

He returned her embrace with warmth, thinking that sometimes women were hilarious and transparent.

"Well, do I?" She cuddled beneath him, fitting the curves of her body to his.

"Do you what?" He might as well enjoy it and play along.

"Do I feel *empty*?" The question in her eyes was playful.

"Now sweetheart, what exactly do you mean? I can arrange for whatever fulfillment you need."

The color rose in her face. She pulled him to her.

"Okay, that sounds all right to me." She reached over to extinguish the bedside light. Thankfully, the boys' room adjoined theirs by the wall on the other side of the room.

After New Year's Day, the family returned home to the Crescent City, finding everything in excellent order. Both businesses were running so smoothly that Michael and Sally could not resist congratulating themselves for having such great people around them. It made sense, they decided, to formalize the roles of both Hambone and Martin, providing more personal time for the two of them. Sally teased Michael about something that had begun to bother her increasingly.

"Don't you see that there's something wrong with this?" Her eyes twinkled.

"What do you mean? We talked about this once before, just not at length." Michael looked carefully at her. He couldn't quite figure out what was with her.

"Okay, Michael. When we go to Fouchet's office to draw up formal documents that put the two of them in their new roles, I will note that Martin Jiles is the Manager of *Café Petite Rouge*. What are you going to list for *MT Entertainment*?"

Michael looked at her with a continually puzzled expression on his face. He considered her remarks carefully.

"Well, Hambone…" He stopped.

"Exactly. Don't you think that we need to start calling this man by his God-given name? At least we need to know his name so that we can put it on paper." Sally laughed.

Michael realized that he didn't know Hambone's name. He did know that he was called 'Hambone' because of his childhood ability to perform a complex, rhythmic thigh- slapping routine to the musical chorus, "Hambone, Hambone, have you heard?" Jeff had told him that the group of boys would regularly perform for the tourists in the French Quarter on weekends. All whistled, most danced, but none of them could handle the rhythm like Hambone could. The coins and even bills would rain into the containers as he became more and more skilled at the routine. Eventually he was simply called by that name. He recounted the story to Sally and assured her that the oversight would be handled. As always he could count on her to handle the necessary details. He reminded himself that they couldn't be a more complementary team.

Jonah 'Hambone' Williams was formally named as Michael's manager. He appreciated the increase in salary, as well as the responsibility. It proved that Michael and Sally bore him the same respect that he had for them. He and Janette had found a nice house on Rue Dauphine near the French Quarter. It was close enough to the club to be convenient for his job. This was his first formal employment outside of actually playing music. His adult life had been focused on making music, but he had readily stepped into the business of booking the groups. His intimate knowledge of the business and many contacts came in quite handy performing the tasks associated with his new position.

Jonah felt that Michael had been his savior in many ways. The northerner had first been the stabilizing factor in the musical group, even though Jeff Arnaud was their acknowledged leader from childhood forward. When they were growing up, Jeff had been different. His good looks and personality pushed him to the forefront. It didn't hurt that his *pason' blanc* grandmother gave him everything he wanted. She had sent Jeff away to college in Ohio. He had barely been allowed to graduate because of some scandal with a girl. Jeff had enlisted in the Army rather than come home and face the questions. Her death came while he was in basic training, leaving him all her assets, including her house near St Bernard and Galvez Streets. Even now, Jeff was always in some kind of scrape. The entire group of them would be affected by whichever current problem he had. Michael came and provided a counter to that instability. More than once Jeff had made the money disappear, but when Michael started handling the booking, all of that changed.

Martin Jiles was a new man. It seemed that Sally's demonstration of faith gave him the final impetus toward positive changes in his life. Janette reported that he was actually courting a woman in the choir at church. The lady was a schoolteacher who looked enough like him to be related. There were rumors of an engagement. Confirmation came one spring day when Martin came in and asked Sally for time off. Since he had never taken a day off in the years that he had worked for her, Sally almost fainted. Happily she gave him an entire month with pay when he explained that he was getting married. Janette was hired to fill in during his absence. It was a perfect solution for all involved.

Sally woke up to an odd sensation. Something did not feel right. Sitting up, she couldn't decide if her discomfort was physical or emotional. As she looked over she saw that Michael still slept comfortably on his pillow. From the foot of the bed, she picked up the lightweight robe and slipped it on as she padded barefoot down the hall. Both boys also lay quietly sleeping in their room. Sally could not shake her feelings of misgiving. Her first inclination was to call her father, but it was a bit early even for him. At first, Rene had resisted her installation of the telephone in his house. Even now, he felt that it was primarily to be used in emergencies, possibly because people from his community showed up at his door to use his telephone as though it was a public service installation. If she called him at such an hour, he would likely assume that there was a tragedy of some kind. Going back to retrieve her slippers, she went to the kitchen and started a pot of coffee. When the rich, dark liquid began to perk, the pungent aroma wafted across the room. She jumped up and ran to the bathroom. There was barely a chance to kneel in front of the bowl before she violently expelled the contents of her stomach. As the ridges of the cold octagonal tiles imprinted her knees, she began to understand. The first sign had been the tenderness in her breasts, which she dismissed. It just hadn't occurred to her that she might be pregnant. Somehow the ages of her boys had dulled her awareness. Maybe it was a false alarm. How would Michael feel about having a baby? She'd wait until it was a sure thing, she concluded while brushing her teeth. Anything could happen. For now, some more sleep would be nice. She turned off the coffee and climbed back into bed next to her husband.

Michael made the business trip to Chicago in early summer. He was able to conclude his affairs within a stay of two weeks and return home. On the evening that he returned, he found Sally, fully clothed, lying asleep on the bed in the dressing room next to her office. Never in the time that they had been together, had he seen her like this. Her slumber was sound and deep. Beneath her eyes he saw faint bluish crescent shaped smudges. It was late, but the only time that Sally used that bed had been with him. He watched her and dredged up those torrid memories. It dawned upon him that she had been a bit listless before his departure. Including the travel time, it meant that she'd been dragging for more than a month. Tomorrow she was going to go to a doctor because he was taking no chances with her health. More than ever, he realized that she was the center of his life. He moved quickly to her side.

Sally's eyes suddenly opened widely. Seeing him, she smiled warmly then started to get up. Michael leaned forward to kiss her eyelids.

"Now, now. Just lie there. Have you been working yourself to the bone?" He noticed that she was a bit thinner. The weight loss served to accentuate her exquisite bone structure. Her hipbones stood out prominently. Without a doubt, her waist was smaller than ever.

"You are so thin, sweetheart. I was just thinking that I could probably circle your waistline with my hands."

He sat down beside her and did so. Sally looked down at his large hands. The elongated and graceful fingers met above her belly button. She started to giggle.

"You won't be able to do that anymore by my birthday."

He looked closely at her, unsure of her meaning.

"What do you mean, Sally? I don't understand."

He remained very serious, very unsure.

She continued to giggle and put her face to his. The kiss was simultaneously sweet and hungry. She jumped up from the bed, running to lock the door. It was late, but a couple of people were still downstairs in the kitchen. She walked back to him, stripping her clothing with each step. First to fall into a pool at her feet was a slinky red silk chemise. For the life of him, he could not figure this one out. She stood before him, stark naked in a pair of red high heeled shoes. He forgot his questions.

Later they lay cuddled side by side. The flickering light of a kerosene lamp illuminated her face. Michael noticed that the shoes remained on her feet. He didn't want to disturb her by moving. He'd just continue to enjoy looking at her long legs accentuated by those shoes. It was a habit of hers to use the kerosene lamps when they were there together. More than once he asked her to stop using them except for emergencies because they had converted to electricity in the spring. Something about the soft glow gave her comfort, she said. They probably reminded her of her childhood. Her eyes fluttered open.

"Are you awake?" She asked.

"Yes, I didn't want to wake you. Are you okay? I realized that you had been a little shaky before I left for Chicago. Then when I found you lying asleep in here, I was worried."

She was quiet for a moment and remembered that she still hadn't told him. Rolling over to face him, she spoke.

"Michael, you have been such a good father to my children. If I had created my own ideal, I could not have come up with someone better than you are."

He kissed her forehead. Something had been gnawing at the back of his mind. He had been reluctant to bring it to her. Now seemed to be as good a time as any.

"Sally, they're my family now, too. I don't know how you might feel about this, but here goes." He took a deep breath and plunged forward. "The boys have grown up without a father and as far as I see, there does not appear to be any connection to his family at all. How would you feel about my giving the two of them my name? I want them to understand that I really am their father now."

She burst into tears. Her gasps were deep and seemed to go down to her toes. His first thought was that he had made a grave error. He must have misread her. Trying to comfort her, he murmured into her ear.

"Oh, Sally. I am so sorry. I just wanted you to know that I love you all and I…" He held onto her.

She took one deep intake of breath to calm herself.

"No, Michael. Michael, there is no problem. What did I do to deserve you? Let's speak to the boys together about adoption. It's their decision. But truly, I believe that they will be very excited."

"Whew! I was afraid that I had insulted you. I know that you loved Bernard very much…" He stopped because she put her finger up to his lips, shushing him.

"Michael, shut up. I was a child when I loved their father. I am a woman now. You, Michael Tolliver, are the man of my dreams. And this gift is a little late for your birthday this year, but… Since you want to be a real father, how do you feel about adding another one to your brood? In time for the next birthday?"

He put his hand on her belly. She was so thin. It just couldn't be.

"Are you saying…?" He looked at her, questioning.

"Yes, I am." She started to giggle again. "We should have a baby in early October. I think it happened that last night at the hotel in New York."

It was Michael's turn to cry. He enfolded her in his strong arms and smothered her face in kisses.

Michael insisted that she see a doctor immediately, he worried that she was so thin at five months along. In fact, her figure was curvier than ever. Only her breasts were fuller and more voluptuous. The next day, Dr. Breaux confirmed her timetable and allayed Michael's fears. In fact she was extremely healthy. He prescribed some of the new vitamin formulas and advised her to drink milk. Sally insisted that he not tell anyone the news yet. Michael respected her wishes, but everyone noticed that he was even happier than usual.

Michael took the boys fishing alone. As the day wore on, he spoke to them about how much he valued being their father now. When he asked if they would have objections to his adopting them, the two boys looked at one another. They could not believe their luck. The family visited Fouchet and started the process.

Sally had written a letter to Carrie herself. In reasonable detail, she told her how she had given Michael the news of her pregnancy when he had asked permission to adopt Bernard and Antoine. She also hoped that Carrie had no objection to his adopting them. When Carrie read the letter, she began to make definite mental plans. Maybe next summer she would retire and go. They would need her assistance then. There was no reason for Sally to be saddled with care of the baby when she had those businesses to run. Besides she wanted to be there to share in loving that baby.

On Sally's birthday, Michael brought to her the completed contract for the purchase of the hotel. Andre' Fouchet had called and told him that everything was finally done. Their offer and deposit had been accepted. The building was now theirs. Finally, she had begun to 'show' just the slightest bit. She was eight months pregnant and men still turned their heads as she passed. After the initial sickness, Sally had carried the baby well. As long as she was dressed, it was really almost impossible to know that she was expecting a baby. Michael could not believe how lovely his wife was. He could barely contain his imagination, as thoughts of the child filled his head. His and Sally's child would be the culmination of their love. Recently he had even pulled out the song that he started for Sally when their romance began. A few bars were added here and there. He seldom touched a piano now, but lately he did play because she asked. Whatever Sally asked, Michael did.

That night, they decided to go to *The Reserve* for a moment of celebration. They laughed because she put on the dress that she wore the first night they met. It fit with a slight difference, but it still looked fabulous since the swelling of her breasts camouflaged the gentle tumescence of her belly. Her body's new curves made the dark silver dress even sexier. When the couple entered the club, Enrico Barone was the first person to see them. He found an excuse to go over and speak to Michael, making sure that Michael was aware that he was now his liquor supplier. There were rumors that the Volstead Act would soon be repealed. Barone wanted to be sure that he got his share of the pie before it was over. Even though he was speaking to Michael, Barone just couldn't keep his eyes off of Sally Tolliver, especially her cleavage. The woman absolutely glowed. He hadn't seen such a combination of animal magnetism and elegance in one female package. Enrico's straying eyes did not go unnoticed by Michael, who was most often tolerant of the looks that other men gave his wife. After all, he felt extraordinarily blessed. However, something about this man made his skin crawl. Sally sensed that all was not right tonight when Michael took her arm and guided her to the door. She had no objection because it was just past her normal bedtime anyway. The man had not been a source of interest, so she missed the reason for Michael's concern.

Emilie Carintha Tolliver was born on October 12th. She named the girl after her mother and Michael's grandmother. Sally had never even entertained the possibility of a real female child. Instead she had presumed that it would be a boy. Her first thought was that she knew nothing about girls. What in God's name was she supposed to do with her? Michael, on the other hand, was captivated. When he saw his daughter, he could not believe his eyes. Emilie was born with thick, straight black hair that grazed her shoulders. The first time that he saw her, she looked straight at him with eyes that were almost gold in color. He guessed that the proper term was some shade of hazel. Circling them were thick eyelashes of sooty black, so long that they touched her eyebrows. A healthy baby, her birth weight was over eight pounds. He could see that she would have long legs, like both of them. Dimples creased elbows, cheeks and knees of a smooth ginger color. He could not help but notice how much she resembled Antoine. His angel was what she was. Her brothers seemed to feel the same way. They stood near the ruffled bassinette and stared for long periods of time.

Cora, Sally's cousin, crafted an entire layette for the new baby. Her own dreams of having a child had receded into the mists, so she took the opportunity to sew all the dainty layette items that she had imagined. The baby slept in a bassinette so luxurious that it seemed fit for a princess. Cora had long ago sewn the very special lining and coverlet for the child that she had lost.

Sally continued to be somewhat overwhelmed with the idea of a little girl. Her experience had not prepared her for the precious little creature that had emerged from her body. Sally held her and looked at her for hours. All that she could think of was that life was not easy for females. The world was slanted in favor of men and it was so hard to get around the stumbling blocks. Without question, the girl would be grow up to beautiful. The promise was clear in her exquisitely aquiline features, her eyes and hair. She prayed that her daughter would not have to suffer as many fools she had. She was so surprised at Michael's attitude. It would seem that he would have wanted a son. One evening when they sat in the bedroom, she finally had to ask. He was holding Emilie, just staring down at her.

"Michael, I know that you must have wanted a son. Perhaps we could try once more…"

He looked up at her. His eyebrows were arched in a querulous manner.

"What on earth are you talking about? Why would I have preferred another son to this precious angel? We have two sons already. If you want to have another child and we are blessed enough to do so, fine. But I would think that we are just perfect now." He resumed staring down at the baby.

Sally sat. Where on earth did this man come from? Really, how had Carrie Tolliver shaped him into such a perfect human being? Again, Sally gave her thanks to God.

In two months, Sally was ready to resume her duties. During her confinement, Michael had ferried the books home to her. Everything was going well, but she simply felt better when she could see things in person as well as black and white.

Martin Jiles was doing a bang up job. His personal life had become extremely interesting. To the shock of everyone who knew them, Martin and his wife produced a son, Alexander Martin Jiles, less than six months after their marriage. The bouncing baby boy was all that Martin could talk or think about. Like Martin, he was fair with green eyes and dark blonde hair. Michael had teased him privately when the baby arrived. He bought Martin a box of cigars. Putting his arms around his shoulders, he whispered in his ear.

"Martin, my man. I say you fooled a lot of people."

"Stop it, Michael. What…" he was blushing uncontrollably.

"Marty, not only were you busy, you were busy making a big old boy!" He slapped the manager heartily on the back. Martin started to laugh himself. He knew that people often underestimated his manhood. Alex was his legacy. He stood a little straighter these days. His life was good.

Another girl from the country came to live with the Tollivers. A distant relative of Sally's family, she was to serve as Emilie's caretaker and all around household help. Sally felt that it was a ridiculous expense. Her father and Michael made all of the arrangements without her knowledge. Not having given a great deal of thought to the whole thing, Sally had entertained some vague idea of setting up a second nursery in her office at the café. Michael reminded her that the hotel would be requiring equal attention. His first desire was that she took more time off. When Sally wouldn't hear of it, he found the girl to serve as help. Her father came into town one day and delivered Anne Marie Toulouse to the Tolliver home.

It was rapidly becoming clear to all of them that the growing household required more room. Michael began searching for a bigger house. The third bedroom was serving both as nursery and a bedroom for Annie. Sally had mixed feelings about having full-time help. Eventually, it became clear to her that she could help the girl in more ways than just employing her as a domestic. When Annie stepped in one day and set Sally's hair in the waves that she favored, the answer was there. Upon her employer's questioning, Annie expressed a desire to one day be a hairdresser. Sally worked out an arrangement for her to go to school at night and acquire the training that she would need to pursue such a career in the future.

Everyday Antoine came home and spent time with his little sister. In his mind, Emilie was the most beautiful baby in the world, an absolute miracle. Annie was skeptical at first that a boy of that age would maintain such an interest in a baby. To her amazement, he took the time to help with feedings and could even burp the baby efficiently. Bernard was not the patient, hands on, kind of brother that Antoine was. He often did spend time visiting with the baby girl, but observation was more Bernard's style.

Whenever time came for piano lessons, Michael had no difficulty finding Antoine. He was sure to be perched on the bench waiting for his father. The boy had progressed at an astonishing rate. While he was an accomplished pianist, Michael felt that the time had come to provide Antoine with greater opportunity. With the help of Andre Fouchet, he found a retired music professor to take over Antoine's training. Dr. Jacob Fein was a kindly, eccentric man who had taught at universities locally and abroad. He and his wife lived in a house on Gentilly Boulevard. The house was filled with plants and surrounded by flowers. His conservatory was like a garden. Sitting in the midst of numerous varieties of plants, his Grand piano seemed oddly more comfortable. Wary at first, the boy began to look forward to his lessons with the new teacher. After his first discussion with Michael, Dr. Fein had requested that he bring Antoine to play for him. The boy was leery of the white man with the odd accent. After a misstep, he went on to perform brilliantly. The old man sent the boy into the actual garden where Mrs. Fein gave him cookies and milk. The curly-haired lady was as nice as her husband had been and she made good cookies, too.

Dr. Fein agreed with Michael's assessment of Antoine's promise. He gave Michael workbooks and set up a schedule of visits for his twice-weekly lessons. When

Michael explained the new arrangement, Antoine initially felt a sense of loss. The music lessons had been his special connection to his new father. After a prolonged and careful conversation, he felt even more special. Michael loved him and believed in his talent. Nothing could have provided more impetus for the boy to want to succeed.

13

MT Entertainment had acquired contracts to represent a couple of up-and-coming female vocalists. Their addition to the talent roster greatly increased the revenues and activity. Female singers were all the rage. One especially pretty girl from Mississippi had the promise of becoming a big draw all over the country. Even now, she was regularly booked into clubs in New York, Chicago and Kansas City. Michael had hopes that this Mississippi Thrush might be the next Bessie Smith. Critics constantly compared her with the reigning Empress of the Blues. The difference was that this girl could improvise with the jazz bands, as easily as she could belt out the traditional blues tunes. Michael was deeply in the midst of negotiations with a major record company on her behalf. This could be the single biggest break for his latest enterprise.

The Reserve remained the star of the MTE holdings. As the club had grown, so had their needs. The suppliers who originally provided them with illicit alcohol had started to become more difficult in their dealings. Eventually they had found the need to change suppliers. No longer were these men local boys, but some of the east coast transplants who were trying to gain a foothold in the Crescent City. They had quietly wedged their way in among New Orleans' sizeable population of stable Italian merchants. Barone was the most ambitious of these men.

Enrico Barone had jumped at the opportunity to gain some leverage into the most successful colored business in town. Everyone knew that the couple had bought a four story building on upper Claiborne Street. It was rumored that they intended to create a real hotel for colored. Barone had to admire the vision that they had. But his usual business considerations were being obscured by his personal interest in the woman. He had caught a glimpse of her entering into a Canal Street building last week. She was an absolutely delicious package. He had tried to catch her attention each time he had come in contact with her. Unlike most of the women in whom he showed interest, she didn't seem to know that he was alive. He knew that she operated a successful restaurant near the Quarter. Many of the businesses like hers had not been as lucky surviving the onslaught of the Depression. He had been told that perhaps she had made minor adjustments in her menu and staffing, but that the food remained superior. With Mardis Gras approaching, it occurred to him that he might have an opportunity to connect with her. His wife wished to have a party to celebrate carnival, but she had been unable to acquire a suitable location. He would suggest that she approach Sally Tolliver.

When Carla Barone walked into her café, Sally liked her immediately. There was nothing about Carla that suggested that she presumed herself to be doing Sally a great favor by speaking to her. Carla recognized the owner of the café as half of the gorgeous colored couple who owned *The Private Reserve*. The two women were close in age and quickly found common ground. Carla remembered the fur coat that Sally wore the night they met, remarking on its beauty. When she complimented her, Sally told her how the coat had been perfect during the New York trip. Carla was originally from that city and was interested that Michael had also grown up there. After consideration, Sally ended up rejecting Carla's proposal to rent out her entire establishment for the Mardis Gras party. The two women, however, ended their conversation as something close to friends.

Sally did assist Carla in making arrangements to have the party at the Barone home. She had considered branching out into catering and this was an opportunity to dangle her foot into the waters. Over the next few weeks, Carla made several visits to Sally's office. At times, Sally felt that the other woman was bending over backward to make her feel less like she was providing a service and more like they were embarking on a grand adventure together. Carla genuinely liked Sally and she enjoyed visiting her well-appointed office in the restaurant. She admired the other woman's busy life. As she gained a perspective on the breadth of Sally and Michael's business interests, her admiration grew.

Carla understood that colored people faced obstacles that she did not totally understand. Her insight, however, had some basis in her own family roots. Her parents were first generation Americans and had faced the challenges of language and culture. Carla's mother had worked beside her father to assure the family's survival. At this point, both Carla's children were in school and she had full time household help. Carla felt that she should do something useful. Most of the women of her circle volunteered at the hospital or did other charity work. These activities did not appeal to Carla Barone. After coming into contact with Sally, she started to get another kind of idea.

The first time that Carla sat down to consider her possible options, she came up blank. Sally had inspired her to believe that she could also do something real with her life. For some reason, she did not discuss her thoughts with Enrico. Her handsome husband was somewhat old fashioned. Carla loved him, she supposed, but for all practical purposes, her marriage had been arranged. Her family was fresh from the old country when Carla was born within months of their arrival.

Her father was a skilled tailor who found a generous clientele among the dapper young men of the gangs in his new country. As she grew up, pretty Carla attracted the interest of those same men. Fearing for the safety and reputation of his daughter, Guido Conti had agreed to an arranged marriage to the son of one of the major crime bosses who believed in traditional values. Carla Conti had been sheltered all of her life. Enrico seemed to sweep her off her feet. She'd had no idea that it was set up. Enrico knew that he got a good girl with old country upbringing. That she was a lovely girl also did not hurt.

Carla was a lovely petite, dark eyed woman. Her mane of thick, coffee colored hair was her best feature. Enrico had immediately been smitten with her, and as an obedient son, he agreed with his father's request and married her. He took a job in his father's organization and ended up handling the southern interests. He was the same kind of husband that his father had been. Occasionally his eye strayed, but he felt that his infidelity had nothing to do with his home life.

Carla's Mardis Gras party was a great hit. She came to visit Sally afterward to acknowledge how great the food had been and how she appreciated all of her help. Sally had also connected Carla with Cora to assist her with the décor for her party. Everything had been uniquely beautiful, Carla reported. Among the special things that Cora created were linen napkins embroidered with masks of purple, green and gold. No one present had seen such unique table linens before. Carla hosted the most unique party of the season, thanks to Sally.

As they shared a cup of tea, Carla told Sally of her thoughts about finding some possible business interest of her own. Sally listened and offered encouragement. After a nice visit, Carla left. Some colorful flowers caught her eye as she descended the stairs. Sitting atop the

Baby Grand piano, the bouquet was striking. Later that afternoon, something occurred to her. Carla realized that she had been analyzing the arrangement and knew what would have made it just a little more pleasing to the eye.

Another of the major impact items at her party had been the group of floral arrangements that she had devised using feathers and masks attached to sticks. Her friends were always asking for her help when it came time to do their flowers. Carla began to consider how her interests could affect her future possibilities.

Two weeks later she found herself in the vicinity of the café and went in to have lunch. Looking around, she was again entranced with Sally's business. How much fun it would be to do such a thing every day, she thought. Dreams of being involved in a prosperous enterprise of her own filled Carla's head. She was so carried away that she was not aware when Sally walked up to her table.

"Why, hello Carla! I wasn't told that you were here."

Carla emerged from the daydream abruptly, embarrassed and feeling like a mischievous child.

"Oh! Hello. I just popped in for lunch. Everything is so nice here. Won't you have a seat?" Her cheeks were flushed and her eyes bright.

"Why, thanks. I didn't mean to disturb you. Was everything to your satisfaction?"

Sally was impressed that the white woman was just as friendly in public. Often behavior varied in private and public encounters between people of different races.

"Of course, your restaurant is marvelous. I had an idea as I was leaving here the last time. Do you have a moment to talk?"

"I'd be glad to talk. Would prefer to go up to my office to have coffee and possibly dessert?"

"The coffee would be fine. Let me just take care of the check."

"I'll have them bring it upstairs. It isn't a problem."

The two women rose and Sally gave instructions to the waiter who approached them. As they went up the stairs, Carla noticed that the view of the room as they ascended the staircase was quite impressive.

"It must make you feel good to look around at your own business especially as you go up these stairs."

Sally thought for an instant as she unlocked the door and showed Carla into her office.

"I hadn't thought of it exactly like that, but yes I do feel a sense of accomplishment."

"Sally, I admire your accomplishments. Like I told you before, I want, no, need to do something real. When I was leaving that day, it occurred to me that I love creating with flowers. Do you think that I might be able to find something in that field? I mean, do you think that it would make sense?"

There was a word that Sally had learned that fit this situation. *Serendipity* referred to a time when things came together to create a perfect set of circumstances. This was such a time. Sally had acquired silent interest in the flower shop, ***Leoni's***. The owner was seeking to retire soon and no one in his family was interested in taking on the mantle.

"Actually, I might be able to help you in that regard."

She only gave Carla the attorney's information. Even though their developing relationship appeared to be solid, Sally didn't want to test it that completely. One lesson she had learned well was that sex and money were better left out of friendships. When Carla left that day, Sally placed a call to Andre' Fouchet and told him about her referral.

The attorney explained the general situation of the owner's plight to Carla Barone when she visited his office. He needed to sell the business quietly because he did not want to damage his client relationships. Fouchet advised her, also, that his nameless investor client would probably be amenable to some flexibility in a purchase agreement. His suggestion was that she complete some sort of an internship under Mr. Leoni's tutelage if the two of them were compatible. From the minute that he took her to the shop, Mr. Leoni loved her. Her plans were off and running.

Once her children were off to school, Carla Barone began her day. Enrico left his home every morning directly upon rising. Carla was aware that he breakfasted daily with a group of his business associates at a restaurant on Carondelet. She couldn't quite understand the reason anyone would need to eat out every morning, but it got him out of her hair. Once she began going to the flower shop, his absence was truly appreciated. She loved to be in when the daily orders from the flower mart arrived. For some reason, the array of varied colorful blooms satisfied Carla's spirit in a way that she had never experienced before.

14

The hotel was well on its way. Michael had found an architect to bring their vision to reality. The young man had listened carefully to Sally and Michael articulate their vision. He used good design principles and practical application to create the ideal plans for the building renovation. When Michael brought the man to Sally's office the first time, she doubted that he would be able to understand her concept. He seemed like such a formal person. A possible explanation was that he had just recently returned home after graduating from a university in Europe. Sally felt insecure when the two of them discussed Paris, London and the things that they had seen there. The young man asked questions, took notes and left with the building plans. When he presented his own drawings, Sally was in awe. Not only had he understood her every wish, but also he had added features that she found perfect. The couple approved the plans and hired the young man to serve a dual role supervising the project. The hotel was one step closer to becoming a reality.

Around the same time, Michael found what he thought to be the ideal home for his family. Not far from where they lived, Michael found a large house that had belonged to a man named Binetti. The man had owned a corner store and a drug store on Broad Street near Canal. He had been sent to prison two years ago for trafficking in prescription drugs and his wife was now ready to leave town. The large house sat on a corner of Orleans Street and had many possibilities. In what was basically his basement there had been a store and a large storage area. Michael's idea was to convert that area into a studio. He would properly insulate the area from the house and avoid a noise factor. He could also create a practice room for the piano that both he and Antoine could use. Michael seldom had the time to play anymore and sometimes he missed that relationship to music. It was clear to him that he received a vicarious enjoyment from Antoine's talent. His boy was developing into a fine pianist according to Dr. Fein, who took the time to keep Michael well informed. He speculated that if the boy continued along at his current pace, he would be well beyond any student that he had ever taught.

When Michael told Sally that his search for a house had been successful, she listened to his description of the basic information. The square footage and the price sounded fine. Michael's taste was impeccable and this was his project. That night he took her to see the property. When she saw that it was her old landlord's house, Sally was naturally struck by the irony. Mrs. Binetti had once offered to buy the property where the café now sat. She didn't bear any hard feelings against the woman because she had, in fact, been kind to her. Of course she had heard of the family's recent problems and felt badly for her, but that house had always interested her. Sally had to admit that it sat spaciously on its high corner in regal splendor, like the queen of the neighborhood. There was no one there to meet them, Sally noticed. Michael pulled out the keys and opened the door. She didn't think too much about it. He had his own set of rules for dealing with the world, Colored or no. Once inside, she saw that the house was more magnificent than she had imagined. There were high curved ceilings and curved doors. Beautifully wrought crown moldings wound throughout the house. Hardwood floors gleamed in almost every room. Italian marble and tile gave the multiple bathrooms a degree of opulence that she had never seen, especially when coupled with the oversized bathtubs. Sally loved the airy feeling that the transoms created. It occurred to her that this house was certainly perfect for tall people, even though the Binettis were people of average height. Maybe he thought tall. Room after room was found to be just what the Tolliver family needed. There was even a room connected to another by a bathroom. Sally saw these as perfect for the nursery and Annie's room. The boys would be able to have separate bedrooms and there were two other bedrooms, as well. She and Michael would enjoy having a suite of rooms entirely for themselves since the master bedroom had attached a sitting room, dressing room and bathroom. Michael took her downstairs and told her of his concept for the basement area, which was actually the first floor. Accessible only from the side, a terraced front yard disguised its existence from the other angles. Sally noticed how different it looked without the goods and shelves of the grocery store. She was touched when he told her of his plan for the practice room. As Michael described it, Sally could envision it all clearly. Suddenly, she realized that Michael was already in possession of the keys because he had done it again. Standing there in the basement, Sally ran through her possible objections and found that none were really valid.

The club and restaurant were solidly in the black. Café Petite Rouge had long ago paid for its remodel. *The Reserve* was very close to paying for itself. Initial subscriptions had covered the purchase. The monthly fees had come very close to completing the payment for the renovation. Since MTE operated out of that space, Michael charged part of its operating costs to that business entity. The couple believed in living within their means and had turned profits back into the business to get where they were. Only the hotel remained a question.

"Well, what do you think?" Michael turned to her expectantly.

Sally wanted to give him a hard time. Perhaps she should pretend that she hated it, but she found that this time she just couldn't do it.

"I think you know. My reactions were vivid enough. Have you spoken to Charles yet?" She said, referring to the young architect.

Michael looked a little sheepish. The expression on Sally's face was matter of fact. He knew that she knew that he had bought this house.

"Sally, when I saw it…"

His response was like that of a child who had gotten caught being naughty. She didn't want that.

"Michael, this house could not be a better match for our family. There is no question what you felt when you saw it."

"It really was a good deal because it's been on the market for almost two years. When I talked to the owner, she was eager to get rid of it. They moved into a much smaller home out in Metairie. She was in need of cash to settle her husband's legal bills. Some of the money was owed to Andre' and he pointed me toward the deal. You know, I had never seen the "For Sale" sign because it faced the other street."

"You didn't answer my question. Have you talked to Charles?"

"Yes, he came over this morning. We went down to pick up the plans from City Hall."

"All right then. It was a great choice, as always. Everything appears to be well on the way. Michael, I love you." She kissed him on his cheek.

The baby's first two birthdays had come and gone. She was even lovelier as a toddler than she had been as a baby. She walked around the house with the dignity of a small princess, her royalty unquestioned by her father and brothers. Annie adored the child and took wonderful care of her. Sally often looked at her and was absolutely enthralled by her prettiness and self-assurance.

The house was finally about to be remodeled. Charles had been so tied up with the hotel, that the house had taken a back seat. Michael had suggested that they go ahead and move, but Sally chose to wait until everything was exactly right. The music room was a vital part of their home and she did not want the piano in a makeshift area. Living amid the chaos of construction was also not on her list of desirables.

Janette Williams worked for Sally full time now. Catering had really taken off and the holiday seasons were especially busy. She managed the catering division quite effectively, while balancing the needs of her young family. Unlike Sally, she did often bring her son to one of the little offices that Sally had carved out from the unfinished area upstairs. Martin occupied the other. Janette's boy was younger than Emilie and she seldom let him out of her sight. He was her first precious child, born when she was thirty. When she worked at night, Hambone took charge of the parenting responsibilities. He and Martin could often be seen comparing notes on fatherhood. Martin and his wife were happily expecting another child any day now. Sally often recalled the bitter man whom she had hired years ago. She had no way of knowing that his change had begun when observing hers and Michael's romance. In many ways their love had been responsible for change in the lives of many people.

Jeff Arnaud could be seen from time to time drifting into the club. He no longer had a group with whom he played regularly. After Jonah and Michael both ceased actively playing, two others moved into backing one of the vocalists and the last went on to a solo career. Jeff was now what was called a session musician. Whenever someone needed a sax to fill in, he picked up work because, despite his fabled talent, no one depended upon him for very long. Michael, seeing that he looked a bit seedy and run down, got him several weeks work in recording sessions. Jeff came to him after it was over.

"Hey, I was leaving and wanted to say thanks. How are Sally and the kids?" He admired his old friend, though it was always from a distance now.

"They are great. You should come by sometime soon, maybe even this weekend, before I have to leave town. It's been too long. You really must see our princess, Emilie. She's two and a half already."

Michael handed him the picture from his desk. Jeff held the heavy frame and examined the small portrait. In the years that he had known Michael, his friend had found the woman of his dreams and become a very wealthy, successful man. The image he held was that of a handsome, happy family. Jeff had never felt more alone. Shaking his head is disbelief, he smiled down at the picture in his hand.

"Michael, you my friend are blessed. Seems it was just yesterday that we were out there in those streets every night."

Michael considered that alternative for just a single moment. He answered very seriously.

"Yes, Jeff. I know that better than anyone."

Jeff put the picture back in Michael's hand. Then he turned and walked out quickly.

For a long time, Michael sat in the chair behind the desk. The light faded and yet he still did not move. When he finally rose and crossed the room, he still had the small picture in his hand. Slipping it into his jacket pocket after removing it from the frame, he locked the door and left for the day.

When he walked into his home that night, everything in his life held a greater value to him. He kissed Sally who had also just arrived, and held her in his arms for a few minutes longer than usual. She sensed his thoughtful mood and stood quietly with him. Wanting to be certain that all was okay, she looked up and spoke.

"Hard day today? Did the session go all right?"

"Sweetheart, actually, I had a very good day. That girl can sing! Wait until you hear the recording! This is the beginning of something great. I can feel it! The musicians were on it up to the minute that we finished."

Sally knew that there was still something beneath it all.

"Okay, that's wonderful. I know there's a *but* in there somewhere, Michael Tolliver. Do we have some problem that I don't know about? Is everything on schedule with the hotel? I haven't talked to Charles, we've missed one another on site."

"Everything is fine. He said that he did try to call you because he had been missing you. Actually, he has the latest drawings for the music rooms. By the way, I told him that it was fine to stop at the café on Monday morning. He is ready to have the crew start the house as soon as we okay it."

"My morning is not too busy. I was on the telephone with Carla Barone who has been working months with our favorite florist, Mr. Leoni, for just a few hours a day. Her husband doesn't know it yet and she's a little anxious about finally telling him. But she is going to buy the flower shop. When she told me about her interest in flowers, I told her about the shop. Last year when I picked up the flowers myself, the old man mentioned that he planned to retire at the beginning of next year. I introduced him to Carla and the rest is history. She is learning the business end of it now. Cora says that her artistic side is covered. By the way, are we still doing business with her husband? I make the entries for amounts, but I wasn't sure if he was still the supplier."

"Yes, it won't be very much longer. Fouchet says that Prohibition is truly almost over. When that happens we won't be forced to deal with the Barones of this world. That is good news about his wife though."

"Michael, what was wrong when you came home?"

"It wasn't so much what was wrong, as that everything was so right. I had a glimpse to remind me of life without my family. Jeff played in session with the group this week. You know he seems somewhat unstable, down at the heels. I thought about gambling and the chances that I took just hanging around with Jeff sometimes. I was very lucky. I never lost more than I had in my pocket. The music thing gave me something, I grant that. If I hadn't gotten involved with music, I might not have stayed here and I would not have met you. If not for Jeff, I wouldn't have come here in the first place. I was headed to California, where there are supposed to be some opportunities."

Sally considered all that he had recounted.

"First of all, Michael you are a man who makes his own opportunities. I think we were supposed to be together. It was in the stars, something that God intended! It's the only way to explain it. A college educated colored Army officer, a gentlemen from New York..." She deliberately slurred it to say ' Noo Yawk' in a very deliberate drawl. "All I can say is you are mine because God gave you to me and that's it. Buddy! I'm not letting you get away." A throaty laugh gurgled from her. Then kissing him again, she wrapped her arms sinuously about his neck.

"You are making it hard for me to leave you, girl. You know I have to get on that train Monday morning."

"Yah suh," she went back into her routine. "We ain't totally stoopid down heah." She grasped both his arms and shimmied against his body before hugging him ferociously. The two of them shared the hug and another laugh before heading in to greet the children together.

Monday morning at six, Sally dropped Michael off at the train station. He would be away for over a month this time. By going to both Chicago and New York he would save travel time later in the year. Early spring was a good time because the chance of running into really bad weather was lessened greatly and the heat would not have arrived. He liked this time of year back east. It gave him a chance to wear his good wools, given that New Orleans was seldom cold enough for them. He settled himself on the car with the New Orleans *Times-Picayune*, a beignet and the last cup of coffee with chicory that he would have for a while.

Sally met with Charles early that morning. Each time that she came into contact with him, her immediate thought was that he was such a nice young man. Michael had found him through a friend who told him about a young colored architect whom he had used for a project. The Tollivers had made it a point to contract with him at the same going rate that white architects were getting. Michael made phone calls back to New York and locally to be sure that they paid him a fair wage. The hotel would be the perfect showcase for Charles's work, as well as the Tollivers' vision. All of the exterior construction was finished and it was already causing a buzz in town.

Sally and Michael had decided that he should talk to Matthew Dickson when he was in New York. Dickson had served under Michael in France and worked in the hotel business for many years. His efficiency impressed them during their stay in New York a couple of years before. Michael had since run into him on his trips and continued to feel the same way. He had been promoted to manager, but that hotel was being turned into co-op apartments and he would be without a job. If he accepted Michael's offer, he would be asked to come down right away. Sally wanted him to be a part of the operation from its inception. Michael would telegraph her, or telephone and advise her of the answer. They believed and hoped that he would be amenable to the change.

Charles Isaac Guidry sat with Sally to show her the final revision of the plans for her home remodel. Charles really appreciated the Tollivers because they had given him a major opportunity. Unlike a lot of people that he had encountered since his return, they had put their money up front. Never once had they put saving money ahead of the integrity of his design. In repayment, his very soul had been poured into the hotel's plans. Rarely would anyone like him have gotten such an opportunity in his hometown.

By using walled courtyards, Charles created a lower floor that allowed the light to come inside while maintaining privacy on the street level. His design was consistent with the old world feeling in the rooms above.

Sally delighted in the leaded windows and tiled patios shown on the illustrations. Giving her unbridled approval, she sent him on his way. Construction on that project, she felt, could be delayed until the hotel interiors were completed. It was not Sally's desire to overload Charles at the beginning of his career. This way also, there could be continuity in the construction crews. Michael would return in a little over a month to continue his overseeing of the new house remodel.

During the marriage, Sally's prior holdings had remained solely hers. Michael provided a willing ear and whatever assistance she asked of him. *The Reserve* had been set up as a corporation, with Michael and Sally serving as officers. MT Entertainment was a part of that structure. The, as yet unnamed, hotel was to be aligned with the restaurant. Sally decided that the time had come to sit down with Michael and discuss her property. Not that she had actually concealed her worth from him, however it just never really came up. She realized that he had most probably been deliberate in ignoring the extent of her property. When he returned, she would take him to Fouchet for a sit down conference. The old house on Orleans should be mortgaged, or sold, to finance the construction on the new one. As another option, she might liquidate a portion of the fund that started with her original inheritance. Sally had been very careful with her money. It had been safely ensconced in Treasury Certificates. She had lost not one dime during the Depression fiasco. Instead she had been able to quietly acquire additional interests with Fouchet acting as her agent. Some people in the New Orleans business community would be extremely shocked to learn that Sally Langlois Tolliver was the "silent partner" who owned them now. Among her investments was the flower shop that Carla Barone was getting ready to purchase. Sally had always liked the gentle, smiling man who sold flowers to her every week, never failing to be courteous and fair with her. The crash had created a difficult situation when he attempted to finance his retirement with short-term purchase of a high-flying stock. When he lost sixty four per cent of the value of his business, Sally had been the silent partner who rescued him by means of a blind trust creatively structured by Andre' Fouchet.

Knowing that Michael had been equally circumspect with his finances helped Sally make her conclusion. The new house had been purchased out right, thanks to a stock market that had indeed been kind to her husband, providing him with a modicum of disposable income. Michael had put the deed into the safe in her office. Despite his denial, Sally thought that he had probably liquidated most of his own nest egg. She was glad that she insisted that the corporation purchase his house from him when the club was established. Michael was a man who gave constantly. At times, she felt guilty that her personality was not as generous as his. At least some of that would be corrected when he returned.

Sally looked forward to the new house. Finally, Carrie Tolliver would come and live with them. Nothing would make Michael happier than to know that his grandmother was no longer working so hard. Repeatedly he had tried to convince her to come. In her mind, she wanted to work for just another year. It was as though she had set some goal in her mind that she was determined to reach. None of Michael's pleading would change her mind. They had finally relented and decided to respect her wishes. One day soon they would all be together and benefit from the enlarged family group.

Sally had engaged her cousin to work with Helene Beauchamp, the young woman who would be the primary decorator of the hotel's interior. Charles Guidry was responsible for introducing his clients to Helene. Having attended college in Ohio studying art, she had been unable to complete her formal education because of a lack of funds. Once home in New Orleans, Helene found work wherever she could. When Sally discussed her ideas for the interior with Charles, he returned with highly stylized drawings depicting further development of her ideas. When he explained that his fiancée had rendered these designs, Sally asked to meet Helene. Her first impression of the young woman was that an elegant hurricane had hit the room. Everything about her was as breathtaking as her drawings were. Her clothing, her looks and her personality were a joy to Sally. She was as flamboyant, as he was a person of quiet dignity. Her artistic vitality was entertaining to Sally. Immediately upon meeting her and discussing the plans, Sally thought that this woman's talent could be an asset to the project when coupled with Cora's considerable skills and practical knowledge. Once again, Sally's judgment proved to be astute. The two women melded into a perfect team. Design boards for every aspect of the hotel project were promptly completed and subsequently approved.

15

Once her children were off to school and Enrico had departed as usual, Carla Barone began her day. Nothing was more exciting to Carla than the early morning visits to the flower market. She loved to meander up and down the rows of brilliantly colored blossoms, choosing any special items needed for the shop. At first, it was enough just to be around when the truck arrived with the regular order of stock flowers from the nursery. As she helped Mr. Leoni unload the boxes, her sense of anticipation never flagged. Opening them far surpassed any past Christmas morning. It was as though each color, each shape, each glorious smell was a personal gift for her. After seeing her obvious pleasure, the old man surprised her one morning.

As she walked into the darkened workroom, Gianni Leoni looked up from the steaming mug of coffee on his cluttered worktable. Strewn about the surface were the remnants, bits and pieces that he used to magically create the bouquets and arrangements for which he was so respected in New Orleans. A rainbow of spools of ribbons in multiple widths and textures were attached across the top of the shelf, while the glint of specialty tools could be seen on the lower shelves within his hand's reach. His first thought was that Carla had become like a daughter to him in these recent weeks. Her arrival into his life had been a glorious thing. Not only was she going to take the reins of the shop, but he felt that it was truly a labor of love for her, as it had been for him. He stood to greet her in his usual courtly manner.

"*Buon Giorno, cara mia.*"

Carla smiled to hear his usual Italian greeting. She and Enrico never spoke the language at home. His justification was that he wanted the boys to be completely Americanized and to speak English without accents. Nothing about his argument made sense to Carla. It would not have hurt if they spoke the language at home sometimes. Her parents had done so and Carla and her sister understood and spoke both languages without accent. She felt that the boys were missing an important part of their heritage.

"It's a beautiful morning, sir." She answered in Italian, happy to hear and speak the lyrical phrases.

"Today, young lady, we are going to go someplace that you will enjoy. My wife will be in the front of the shop until we return. There's a very important order for a banquet at the Hotel Vieux Carre tonight and we will need a few specialty items."

When they arrived at a row of flower vendors in the specialty marketplace tucked away in a quiet corner of the city, Carla was amazed. Being in the midst of the massive profusion of exotic blooms made her feel as though she was physically immersed in a Monet painting, wading through a riot of color. The experience, for her, was reverential. From that day forward, Mr. Leoni passed that task to her.

Shortly after Enrico's departure this morning, she had slipped quickly out to perform her favorite chore. As she made her way thru the vendors in the early mists, she was distracted. Very soon, she would have to explain her plans to Enrico because the transfer of ownership would happen in a short time. Mr. Leoni was ready to go home to his native Sicily. She had spoken to the banker, who assured her that there would be no problem. However, Enrico would have to sign the papers also. She would speak to him after dinner this evening.

On most mornings, the small group of men sat outside to eat. The crowd of people who ate breakfast at *Hanrahan's* daily coveted the tables on the restaurant's garden-like terrace. This specific table was permanently reserved for Barone and his associates when the weather permitted. Currently these men were involved in a frantic scramble to balance their sinking business vessel. The word was that the repeal of Prohibition was on the floor of Congress at the moment. Since the greatest part of their revenue was derived from the illegal sale of liquor, other sources of profit needed to be developed. In a city as sophisticated as New Orleans, these men had operated smoothly. The city did not come to be called The Big Easy without reason. Certainly the atmosphere was no different during Prohibition. Enrico, especially, felt the pressure. His father expected him to create new streams of revenue to support the organizational structure. The younger man intended to counter his father's concerns about the end of the bootleg empire with a well thought out plan of legitimization. He had investigated the requirements for legal distribution of alcohol once the laws changed. His attorneys supported his plans. The problem lay with convincing his father. Enrico would handle that chore in a face to face meeting soon. He welcomed the idea of solely legitimate business dealings. The old ways belonged in the old country and he was not a 'Mustache Pete.' This city was not going to be some battleground like Chicago and New York had become, not if he had anything to do with it. His business associates were in total agreement. If he could tie up his distribution contacts legally, he could continue to operate in much the same manner. He would go to each of his major clients and make arrangements. He would start with Michael Tolliver.

When Barone stopped in at MTE, Jonah Williams listened to his proposal for the possible arrangements with him. He was told that Michael would have to handle any contracts of that sort. Jonah told Barone that he would put him on Michael's calendar after he returned. No one expected the law to change before then. Enrico was told that Michael would return from New York and Chicago in six weeks at the most.

Upon approaching the other major clients, he found that most seemed to be amenable to continuing business dealings with him legitimately. In an even better development, the owner of a large speakeasy up near the Irish Channel offered to sell him majority ownership of his establishment. The man told his plan was to divest himself of his interests soon due to health reasons, so he would gladly sign over the property for a favorable price. Suddenly things were looking even better for him. He would have a firm foundation upon which to base his legitimate business enterprise.

It was a bright spring day and his life was finally turning in the right direction. Enrico thought it a good day to make the effort to treat Carla to lunch. His wife seemed a little out of focus recently. It was not his habit to drop into the house during the day. The house was Carla's kingdom, he believed strongly in that. She had produced his sons and as long as she handled her end of things in an okay manner, he had no complaints. His attempt to take her last week had fizzled. When he arrived home that day, the maid had said then that maybe she was lunching with her lady friends. Most probably, he thought, they ended up shopping on Canal Street. Oh well, what did he care? Usually, spending a few dollars on herself put her in a good mood. This time as he arrived home he saw that the maid was busy in the living room. Walking throughout the house, he couldn't find Carla. After looking in the garden, he returned to the living room a little irritated. The maid must know where she was. Holding up his hand to get her attention, he stumbled over his words because he could never remember the woman's name. Something about her intimidated him, believe it or not. That was Carla's territory, after all. Damn her!

"Excuse me. Where is Mrs. Barone?" He called out to the woman.

The maid, Mary Alice, knew that her employer didn't remember her name. She seldom dealt with him as a conscious choice. Miss Carla was a decent person, but something about that one got on her nerves. She turned to him with her attitude already in place.

"Good day, Mr. Barone. How are you?" She would not tolerate rudeness from anyone.

"I'm fine. I said where is Mrs. Barone?" Enrico was becoming more upset. Couldn't the woman hear?

"Sir, she doesn't exactly have to tell me where she goes, and she didn't."

His face was beginning to turn red now. He was certain that the woman probably did know where Carla was. Turning on his heel, he went into the bedroom and slammed the door.

Mary Alice was glad that she had finished that part of the house. She made it a point to clean the living quarters as soon as Miss Carla left everyday. Her new schedule made it work better that way. By the time that Carla Barone returned, she was usually working on dinner. Maybe the husband would leave again today. This was the second, or third time recently that he had shown up unexpectedly during the day. Mary Alice made a note to herself to remind Miss Carla that she needed to take care of her business.

Enrico was fuming. There was a limit to this crap. Carla had always been pretty predictable. But lately, she was acting differently. He didn't need this. Pouring himself a drink, he turned on the radio. He'd listen to the ball game. By the time that Carla got home with the kids, he had finished more than half the bottle of scotch. Mary Alice told her immediately that Enrico had been home for a long time and that he was probably getting suspicious. Thanking her housekeeper, Carla settled the kids in and got them fed. Finally, she found him asleep in the room. After noticing the bottle, she decided against waking him. He'd be in a better mood after he slept off the alcohol.

The kids were bathed and in bed before Enrico woke up. He looked around him and saw that it was dark already. Amidst the pounding in his head, his anger crept back in immediately. He poured another drink. Where the hell was Carla?

At that moment, Carla walked into the room.

"Hi. I didn't wake you because you seemed to be sleeping so..."

She did not get the rest of her sentence out before he was up in front of her, yelling. His face was distorted and reddened.

"Where the hell have you been?"

This was unlike her husband. From time to time he lost his temper, but this behavior was unprecedented.

"Enrico! What is wrong? Don't I have the right to go out of the house?"

"You have been going out all the time. At least twice, maybe three times lately, I came home and you were not here." He was angry and frustrated.

"I am sorry. Enrico, I didn't mean to cause you any upset. I guess that I need to go ahead and talk to you anyway."

The scotch was roiling in his stomach. He had not eaten since breakfast. It was her fault.

"What are you talking about? Where were you?"

Carla sensed that his state of mind was not good, but she had no choice but to go ahead.

"I have an idea that I have meant to talk to you about. The time just wasn't ever quite right. Also I wanted to be absolutely sure." She went ahead and explained her need to do something useful and finally, the plans for the flower shop. She spoke cheerfully and in an animated manner. Her joy and anticipation were clear.

Enrico could not believe his ears. She was his wife. It was not her place to make a way outside of his home especially without his permission.

"How did you do such a thing?" His face was an ugly, twisted mask. Carla couldn't understand why he was acting this way. Her plans could only benefit the family in the long run. If she was happier, then everyone would benefit.

"But Enrico, it will be good. You will see. I am very good with the flowers. Mr. Leoni says that I am a natural. He's such a nice man, a Sicilian."

"What gave you the idea that you could work outside of my house?" He grabbed her throat, pushing her against a wall.

Carla had never seen him like this. It must be the alcohol.

"You will see, Enrico. It will work. I will be a successful businesswoman like Sally Tolliver...arrghh." Her words ended in a gurgle as he raised her up so that the weight of her entire body was on her throat.

At that moment, Enrico slapped her, once and then again.

"That high yellow bitch put these ideas in your head? Is that what you are saying? You are not some colored trash!" He hit her again and she struggled for breath.

Carla raised her hand to her bloody mouth. As he released her, she slid to the floor. Looking up at the twisted face of the man leering above her, she couldn't recognize him as the father of her children. This was not her husband. He had never before acted that way. She struggled to her feet, straining to speak. Her mind was reeling as she cried out at him in disbelief.

"I don't believe that you are treating me this way. Things are changing. Women don't just stay at home any more. My mother always helped my father in the shop!"

"Helped him, yes. That was different. You are my wife. You don't have to work. You are a Barone woman now! You do nothing without my approval!"

He hit her this time with his fists over and over, raining blows to her face and body. He stormed from the house, leaving Carla in a crumpled heap on the floor.

Still drunk and raging, Enrico Barone drove around. How dare she presume to do something like that without his permission? He would have none of that! Constantly he refueled his rage by repeating Carla's remarks over and over. When he began to notice his surroundings, he thought about Sally Tolliver. That haughty bitch had influenced his wife to act behind his back. The restaurant was ahead. It was almost closing time and it occurred to him that Michael was in New York. Parking carelessly, he went inside and walked past the desk quickly without pausing. The foyer was crowded with the last diners departing. What was left of the staff was preoccupied with cleaning tables. He made his way up the stairs without being stopped. Having observed the general upstairs layout previously, he easily found Sally's office and barged in without knocking. She sat at her desk and calmly looked up as he pushed his way in, immediately calculating the look on his face. He stopped inside the door, breathing rapidly. Her first thought was that he resembled a rabid dog. Clearly assessing the danger factor, she folded her ledger and opened the drawer as if to put it away.

"Mr. Barone, to what do we owe this pleasure?" her voice was coolly controlled as her obscured hands performed their task.

"Pleasure?" He continued to breathe through his mouth. His normal good looks were no longer apparent.

"Is there reason that you are here? And is there some reason why you didn't knock?" Sally was as calm as he was frenzied. Only her hands moved with precision in the center drawer, then rested there.

"Tell me something. I have always wondered about." He looked at her with a sneer that alternated from nasty to lascivious.

"What is that, Mr. Barone?" She would be glad to answer a question and get him out of here.

"I know how things are down here. Looking at you, I have always wondered about something. Tell me, is your daddy white?" he smiled suggestively.

Sally never batted an eyelash in giving him her reply.

"Nah, suh." She dragged out in her best southern drawl.

"My mammy is."

She smiled and drew her hands from the drawer. In them she held the pearl handled revolver that Michael insisted that she keep loaded and ready. The menace in her voice was enough to chill his ardor and begin to sober him up. After cocking the pistol, she pulled the rope chord behind her with her left hand. Enrico barely had time to react before the door opened explosively as two of her waiters came barreling into the room. Because of the hour they knew that something had to be amiss. When the men saw her holding the gun on Enrico Barone, they grabbed him.

"What do you want us to do with him, Ma'am?" the taller of the two men asked. He recognized the man, but Sally was his boss. He would do whatever she said.

"Just show him out and lock the front door, thanks." Sally kept the gun leveled. This was not good, she thought. Enrico was a dangerous man. Tomorrow she would call Michael. While she was not easily alarmed, he needed to know about this. Never having felt that threatened before, it took more than a few minutes before she calmed down enough to put the gun away.

The two men accompanied a surly Enrico down the back stairs. Everybody knew of his connections and both were wary of his presence. No one wanted trouble, but he could not come in there and disrespect Mrs. Tolliver. The younger of the two, spoke to him. He could smell the stench of alcohol coming from the crime boss.

"Mr. Barone, maybe you should go home and get some sleep."

Enrico spat. How dare they treat him this way and as for her, he would handle her in another way. Jerking away from the pair, he went to his automobile. The nerve of her! He went directly to his office and made a phone call. There was more than one way to handle a bitch! How dare she!

He went home. Carla was asleep. He climbed in beside her and soon snored loudly.

The next morning, Carla felt her husband stir. She feigned sleep, remaining in bed. Pain wracked her entire body, raging through every nerve ending. Her mouth was torn in two places. Late the night before, she had seen that her head was badly swollen, her face an ugly collage of black, blue, red and yellow. The sight had frightened her. She had lain as still as possible until real sleep came. Now looking down at her face Enrico felt badly. She shouldn't have made him do that, but she had needed to be taught a lesson. It would be okay now. He'd buy her something pretty to set everything straight.

Early the next morning Sally placed a call to the hotel where Michael was staying. Her recounting of the evening's events gave her husband cause for concern. Remembering the way that the man had looked at his wife before, Michael began to worry even more. He thought it a good idea that he should come home immediately, but she said no because travel was expensive and time consuming. However, she did want him to be aware. She said that she could handle things just fine. Before he left for Chicago Michael decided, he would contact Hambone and have him hire a couple of men to keep an eye on Sally. These guards would be put in place to be sure that Barone didn't come back. Despite his reputation, Sally didn't think that the man's bite was as bad as his bluster. Michael wasn't so sure.

Matt Dickson had accepted their offer and would be arriving next week, Michael advised her. His personal itinerary called for him to leave for Chicago on Saturday morning. He would visit with Carrie once more and then contact her once he arrived in Chicago. After Sally updated him on everything happening at home and on the business front, they hung up.

Tony Barone was Enrico's younger brother. Their father sometimes worried that his oldest son was going soft around the edges, but he bore no such concerns about Tony. In fact, the younger man's ruthlessness scared him at times. Antonio Barone was a classic psychopath. When Enrico placed the call to Tony in New York, his fury was apparent. He would show Sally that she could not get away with threatening him. His first inclination was to send someone to her home, but he didn't wish to muddy his own front yard. His brother relished such a task and put his plan in place.

Tony Barone was driving the taxi when Michael came out to go to the train station. Though it was unusual to see a white driver in Harlem, it was not totally unheard of. A well-placed bribe put him in the proper slot to slip into line and take that particular fare. He had made sure of that. Michael read his newspaper as the cab inched its way through the maze of early morning traffic. New York papers were a pleasure that he missed and enjoyed the chance to read them again. At an intersection, two men jumped into the back of the cab. Peeling rubber, the driver took a sudden turn from the street. The men commenced to beating Michael unmercifully. Outnumbered, crowded and surprised, he was unable to effectively defend himself in the close space. After pummeling him into unconsciousness, they threw his broken, bleeding body into an alley. To add insult to injury, they stripped him of his outer clothing and doused him with liquor. The contents of his suitcase were emptied into a trash bin across town. Any pieces of identification were destroyed.

The police found Michael after he had lain exposed and injured for hours, his condition grave. Because he had no identification, he was admitted into the public hospital. Since he was the third John Doe that day, the admissions clerk capriciously chose to vary his label. *James A. Doe* was unconscious due to pneumonia, a broken arm, numerous contusions and three broken ribs. Varied cuts and facial contusions made his features unidentifiable. He was presumed to be an alcoholic derelict. Due to a clerk's sense of whimsy, his record would not be pulled up later when 'John Doe' searches were made.

Tony Barone called his brother and told him that the message had been delivered. Enrico hung the black telephone on its stand and laughed with evil vicarious pleasure. That would teach that bitch a lesson. And it could never be connected to him. While he did not often resort to violence, it was sometimes a necessity in both professional and personal life. The memory of Carla's bruised face crossed his mind, making him remember that he would have to stop at the jeweler's on the way home.

Upon waking, Carla panicked. She would have to tell Mr. Leoni some lie as an excuse. Something serious, but not too serious would be the answer. It came to her that some of the kids had measles in the area, so she called and made that excuse that Pauly had a fever and a rash. The kindly man offered to bring calamine if she needed, just as he would have done for his daughter. Tears were in her eyes when she thanked him and advised that she hoped to be in sometime in a couple of weeks. Carla then had Mary Alice take the boys to school and tell them that she was sick with something contagious. None of them deserved to see her looking like this. The net of lies caused by her husband's rage got bigger and bigger. Once they were out of the house, Carla called her doctor. When she told the man of her problem, he arranged for her to come into the rear door of his office at lunchtime. Her physical condition was such that Mary Alice had to help her to the car and drive her to the office building, her face obscured by a scarf and hat. After wiring her jaw, the doctor stitched the cuts in her mouth and cheeks. Her body was wrapped to assist her broken ribs in healing. An envelope full of pain pills was shoved into her hand. Salves were dispensed for the other contusions on her body. He knew to whom Carla was married, but he felt compelled to treat her anyway. Mary Alice could not believe the damage that her employer had done to his wife. It wasn't that she hadn't ever seen such behavior. She just hadn't seen it in this house before. She helped Carla into her bed, saying a quick prayer for the petite woman.

A sheepish Enrico came home after the housekeeper had gone. He said goodnight to his children, then went into his bedroom to face Carla, finding that she too had gone to bed. Her plan was to avoid him for long enough to figure her options. He had the present with him and wanted to make things right. Such things happened. She would be okay. He put his hand on her shoulder and shook her.

"Carla, honey?" His voice was gentle and contrite.

His wife had taken sleeping pills in addition to the pain pills to assure herself that she would not have to deal with him. Today she had considered calling her father. She had investigated the price of train tickets for her sons and herself. The household accounts had enough money for only one ticket. Enough jewelry lay in the safe deposit box to finance her get away. But even better, if she could get rid of all of it, including her rings, she could buy the flower shop. The only obstacle was Enrico himself. He had told her how he felt about it. Would he leave her alone if she chose to go ahead with her purchase? She just needed time to think. Enrico saw that she was truly asleep. He tried not to look at her face. Surely it would go away soon. He put the small box in his bedside drawer.

The next morning, Carla's twelve-year-old son came into her room. He was concerned about his mom. She wasn't one to lie around and she was never sick. Brushing her hair, she came walking from the bathroom. Startled by the boy sitting on her bed, she forgot for a moment how she looked.

"Pauly, what are you...?" She saw the terrified look on his face. Running to her, he put his arms around his mother. His head was now above her shoulder.

"Mom, what happened to you?" Tears glistened at the corners of his eyes.

Carla quickly tried to think of a lie. None would come.

"Don't worry about me! Honey, it was just an accident. I'm fine." Her voice was barely understandable through the wires.

The boy was no fool. He put the possibilities together and turned and ran from the room, crying. Carla did not want to involve her children until she absolutely had to. At that moment, Enrico came home, striding into the bedroom with purpose. He had decided that he couldn't put off facing Carla. They needed to get past this.

"Good morning, Carla. I thought that I might catch up with you. How are you feeling?" He came and put his arms around her.

Carla didn't answer him. She stood quietly. Her skin seemed to burn in the places where he touched her.

"Do you hear me, Carla? I am talking to you." He pushed back from her and held her by her shoulders.

"Of course I hear you, Enrico. What do you want me to do?"

There was no emotion in her voice. The words were unclear and it hurt to talk. She felt dead inside.

"Are you trying to be smart with me? I thought we settled this. Carla, you are my wife. You have to know your place."

Not once in all their years of marriage had Carla responded to her husband's anger with such fire.

"Screw you! Do you treat me like a wife? A wife is someone that you cherish. You treat me like dirt!"

She spat at him. Before he thought about it, Enrico swung at her. This time he hit her in the chest, propelling her into the nightstand, sending the lamp to the floor with a crash. Explosions of pain shot through her body. Their son came running into the room. He saw his mother fly across the room and tried to defend her. Enraged, his father swung and hit him in the face. Teeth and blood spewed about the room. Without thinking about anything but her son's well being, Carla grabbed under her pillow. The gun that she drew out in her hand was loaded. The click releasing the safety was an ominous sound filling the room. Enrico turned toward his wife.

"What the hell is with you broads? I'll make you eat that!"

He rushed to take it from her hands. She pressed the trigger. It was not as hard as she remembered. The thunderous sound filled the room, propelling him backward. A crimson flower seemed to bloom in the middle of her husband's chest. His white silk shirt collapsed into his body. Looking at the gun in her hand, she let out a horrible wail and ran to her son. Enrico Barone breathed one last time, but the look of surprise did not leave his face.

After seeing the condition of the woman and child, the authorities chose not to pursue charges against Carla Barone. Enrico's death made the headlines. Sally found it interesting that it came so close upon the heels of her own encounter with him. She placed a call to Michael in Chicago, but he had not checked into the hotel yet. Day after day, she tried. A whole week passed. No, Michael Tolliver had not checked in. Finally, Hambone called her to say that the Chicago contacts had inquired as to why Michael had not kept the appointment. Matt Dickson arrived that same day and had no news of a change in Michael's itinerary to report. Sally had begun to get quietly hysterical. No one knew anything. He had checked out of the hotel, but the railroad could not say if his ticket had been used. Sally called Carrie, hoping that perhaps he had decided to spend additional time with his grandmother for some reason.

When Sally called, Carrie's world dissolved into a red haze as she collapsed clutching her chest. Her last conscious thought was that her God could not be so cruel. Carol Quincy heard the noise when Carrie collapsed and rushed downstairs to her aid. Grabbing the phone, she advised Sally what had happened. As she frantically summoned the family's driver, her realization was that Carrie was more than an employee. For over thirty years, this woman had run her household, as well as been her confidant. During the difficult hours rushing through the New York traffic and then waiting at the hospital, she took complete stock of the relationships in their lives. There had been so much tragedy in the past few years. She had friends who had lost their only sons and husbands during the war. It seemed that so many families that were not touched by the war were then devastated during the Crash. Carol had often remarked to Silas how blessed they had been. But now she was quietly hysterical. After the arrival at the hospital, she had called Sally to update her on Carrie's condition and then called her husband to advise him of Carrie's collapse. Pacing back and forth, she tried to maintain decorum. She rushed to Silas when he arrived. Seeing her state, he enfolded her in his arms, as words poured out in a torrent, explaining what had precipitated the event. Michael had disappeared! The judge was not sure which incident upset him most. Michael was dear to both he and his wife. His disappearance was devastating to them. By now, shadows striped the tepid green painted halls of the hospital. Fewer people circulated about. A doctor emerged from behind the heavy doors at the end of the corridor and looked curiously about the waiting room. He glanced down at the chart as he spoke.

"Are you here for Carintha Tolliver?" His voice was a crisp baritone, surprisingly deep for a man of such slight statute. "I am Matthew French, Cardiology fellow here."

"Yes. We are Silas and Carol Quincy, her employers and friends." He turned to look at his wife, who shook her head in agreement.

Doctor French was aware of Silas's position and influence. Gossip never fails to make its way about the room in an emergency situation. Unfortunately, such information did sometimes influence the level of care received by a patient.

"Judge Quincy, Mrs. Quincy," he nodded his head in acknowledgement. "Mrs. Tolliver is resting comfortably now. She suffered a mild cardiac incident, but we were able to stabilize her. It appears that she is anemic and slightly underweight, which magnified the cardiac issue.

She needs extended rest, iron supplements and a balanced diet."

Carol promptly spoke up, "Doctor, she will receive the best of care and diet. She is a compulsive worker, who always keeps herself busy. I will see that she rests."

The doctor glanced at the judge's wife and wondered if she really cared about the health of this Colored woman.

Some of these society types talked a good game, but acted in an entirely different manner when in the privacy of their homes.

"Her recovery should be complete if she follows these instructions when she is discharged. I feel that she should remain here for a week." He gave a sheet of paper to Carol, who immediately began reading.

"Doctor?" Silas looked at the physician carefully.

"You do understand that we expect Mrs. Tolliver to receive the best of care. She is very important to us. I would like her to have a private room."

The doctor made a note on his clipboard and asked the pair to come with him. He led them down to the charge nurse's desk, where he gave the orders for Carrie's care, including the request for a private room. At this order, the nurse's eyebrows raised in question as she stole a glance at the couple accompanying the doctor.

"If you would like, you may see the patient as soon as she is moved to her room. If there are any questions, feel free to contact me, Judge Quincy. Nurse McMillan here will come and get you. Judith, please take care of the transfer."

Judith McMillan rose and bustled down the hall wondering what these people were about, they certainly seemed to be genuine. She couldn't help but think that the Tolliver woman was lucky to have been admitted on Matthew French's shift. In fifteen minutes, the nurse returned and ushered Silas and Carol to a cheery room on a side corridor.

Carrie lay propped among the pillows looking gray and wan. Though the nurse had told them that she was conscious, nothing about her manner suggested it. Silas placed his hand on her arm and spoke to her quietly.

"Carrie? Can you hear me?" He asked.

She did not respond. Inside her semi-conscious state she heard him, but she knew that if she opened her eyes, she would have to face something dark and ugly hovering about the edges of her mind.

Carol understood that Carrie was hiding from the day's events. Once long ago, she had experienced that kind of pain. If she let herself fall into it, the deep, dark place to which she sank after her last miscarriage still beckoned after all these years. Considering Carrie's personal history of loss, Carol Quincy sometimes wondered how she remained so optimistic. Now she remembered that Michael had been the key to Carrie's happiness, and that key had vanished.

The couple sat in the room for a while. Carrie simply lay quietly with her eyes closed. Nurse McMillan came in to advise that visiting hours were over. As they left, Silas asked her to inform them promptly if there was a change.

As the Carol and Silas Quincy descended to the lobby, both were lost in private thought. Sam, the driver, retrieved the car and got them home in a hurry. Carol prepared drinks and they sat in the leather chairs that faced one another across the desk in Silas's study. She broke the silence first.

"Darling, a lot of things ran across my mind today. I mean when I came downstairs and found Carrie, it was very upsetting. Then I realized that I have spent as much time with Carrie over the past thirty-eight years as I have with you. I also realized that she and Michael are extremely important to our lives, to us." She gazed into the sparkling amber liquid in her glass.

Silas couldn't believe how much in tune the two of them were. He chuckled as he rose, walked around the desk and kissed her forehead. Kneeling in front of his wife, he looked into her eyes as he spoke.

"It is often difficult for me to phantom how in sync we are as human beings. I love you dearly, Carol. And I am reminded instantly when you express my very own thoughts aloud. In all the ways that matter, we truly are one."

She smiled back at him. At least she had the perfect husband. It occurred to her that they hadn't updated Sally Tolliver on Carrie's condition. "You should call Michael's wife and let her know that Carrie should recover nicely according to the doctor. I am simply not up to it right at this moment. Tell her don't worry we will look after Carrie, she's like family. And Silas, please don't forget to let her know that we are here for her, also."

The judge wondered to himself why women presumed to be the arbiters of kind expression. Carol never failed to ask him to parrot her words. When Sally's telephone rang, she picked it up in the middle of the first rrring. Her voice sounded desperate, "Hello?"

"Sally? This is Silas Quincy. My wife and I just returned home and wanted to advise you of Carrie's condition."

Her reply was thankful, "Oh, bless you both. Today has been… Well, you understand. Please tell me that she's going to be okay. I just don't know what…"

"My, dear please listen," Silas interrupted her. His voice was soothing and gentle. "I can only try to imagine what you are feeling. First of all, Carrie is resting. The doctor expects that she will recover completely. She will need care, but she is our family and we will provide it.

Surely this business with Michael is some kind of a mistake. It makes no sense at all. I will have someone look into the situation here. Michael is a decent man, a man of substance. He can't just vanish."

They talked for some time, but his words did not really comfort Sally. 'At least', she thought selfishly for a moment, ' Carrie will be cared for. Who will care for me? Only Michael was there for me and he's gone.' Tears came rolling down her face, as she sat with her hand on the silent telephone. 'Any minute now, any minute it will be a mistake. Have someone call and tell me that it was a mistake,' she pleaded to God. Sally sat in her office for hours. The shadows of the evening lengthened. She couldn't move, think nor cry. 'What in God's name could have happened to him?' She was afraid to leave the phone for even a moment. She worried about poor Carrie. She worried about herself and her children.

The staff went home for the evening, leaving her there as they often did. Sally finally went into the dressing room and tried to sleep for at least part of the night. By dawn she was back at her desk, staring at the mute black instrument. In the morning, Hambone came to the café. He had gone by the house on the previous evening and waited, but Sally never came. Dragging himself, he went home to let Janette know what had happened. When he awakened, it occurred to him where he would find her. Jonah arrived at the same time that the cleaning team came and bounded up the stairs. His grace and quickness would have surprised many because of his size. He knocked at the door and entered simultaneously. Sally looked up at him and burst into tears.

"Did you hear anything?" He asked as he put his hand on her shoulder.

"Nothing. No one has seen him since he checked out of the hotel. As a last resort, I called Carrie. Hambone, she had a heart attack when I told her that he had been missing for over a week."

"Sally, I called the police in Chicago, too. Nothing could be found. Nobody has a record of anything concerning Michael Tolliver anywhere."

"Maybe he had an accident," she was grasping for straws. "Did you think of that?"

"Yes, Sally. Nobody anywhere knows anything." His eyes were teary, his face worn. "There is no record of Michael Tolliver, neither is there a John Doe victim fitting his description."

The big man tried to convince Sally to go home. She could not face the house. Everything there would remind her of Michael. He tried to convince her that he should go to Chicago and look for his friend and employer. Sally would not hear of it. There was Janette and his son to think of.

Days had grown into weeks, then months. Sally operated inside of a shell that nothing could penetrate. She didn't know what to say to the boys. Not knowing what to say, she said nothing. They then, were more lost and confused than Sally herself was. The silence was deafening. Emilie was another problem. The little girl looked for her daddy because she was accustomed to spending time with him daily. Whenever Sally looked into her serious little face and saw the question there, her heart broke again and again. Cousin Cora asked to let her help by caring for Emilie until Sally could determine some things about her life. Knowing that she was of little use to her children right now, Sally agreed reluctantly. The boys had been alone before and they were big boys now. Her focus became trying to restore some normalcy to their lives. She spoke to Dr. Fein, who agreed to have his wife pick Antoine up on lesson days. Daytime classes in Beauty Culture were arranged for Annie. She made excuses to

Bernard for discontinuing his time at the café, not wanting him to see her in such turmoil.

Sally buried herself in her business, reviewing and updating menus. No mundane task was undone. She kept in touch with Carrie in New York. The older woman was recuperating nicely, but her spirit was extremely crushed. Carol and Silas Quincy made every effort to keep in close contact. His attempts to find out anything about Michael's disappearance came to naught. Despite his contacts, no new information had been uncovered. Michael Tolliver had checked out of his hotel on schedule and disappeared like a wisp of smoke. The doorman recalled seeing him enter a cab, but no one remembered which company. None of the companies had a record of the fare so there the trail stopped.

The many details of the hotel were magnified to absorb all of her time. *The Reserve* needed more of her attention since Michael was not there. Hambone had stepped in to the booking and talent management with both feet. Sally had to remind him to go home to his family. The club was not her favorite place. It was a different place without her husband at her side. Men noticed her more there. With a drink or two under his belt, everyman thought he was Romeo. Many of the newer clientele were not accustomed to the sight of the beautiful long legged woman striding across the floor. One man had the nerve to touch her. Sally never paused. She swung a full-blown right hook at his shocked face, before he was able to dodge or duck. The moment became legend in the lore of the club. Her bouncer dragged him out and dumped him in the street. No one ever presumed to touch another woman in that club.

16

Cora adored the little girl. Her degree of enjoyment in caring for Emilie made her almost feel guilty. She was such a beautiful and serious little thing. Despite the tragedy, Cora loved having responsibility for her cousin's baby. Something seemed to warm her very soul these days. She knew that Sally would want her child back sooner or later. But until that day, Emilie was welcome in the Rolande home. Her heart had gone out to Sally whose pain was apparent to everyone around her. Months had passed with no word of Michael. It was as though he had vanished off the face of the earth.

As the months passed, Cora noticed that she had progressed into another stage of her life. It was a bit early, but so be it. The whole process was not functional in her life anyway. She just dreaded the other things that came along with it. Hot flashes and night sweats were not something to which she looked forward. Her husband noticed it first and came to a different conclusion. He realized that he had been a little too happy and relaxed. A mistake must have been made. When she said nothing, he tried to dismiss his concerns. They had been through so much.

He did not want her to hurt any more, either physically or emotionally. As her body began to thicken, he waited for her to say something. Then he realized that she, too, had been distracted by the presence of the child. On the day that she first felt movement and recognized it for what it was, she almost jumped out of her skin. Her body had experienced that sensation before. The joyful realization of her condition flooded her whole being. When her body became significantly larger, they were afraid to speak of it even to each other. It was as if saying it aloud might cause it to disappear. Albert touched her expanding belly with reverence and joy. They prayed together for God's continued blessings without daring to be specific. Caring for the little girl was so much of a joy that they pretended that nothing else was happening. When the sixth month passed, they began to be very hopeful. Because of her past history, she reluctantly went to the doctor, who summarily scolded her for delaying the visit. Many women gave birth to a child safely in their mid-thirties he assured her. After all, it was not her first pregnancy he reminded Cora and Albert. They made a pact to say nothing to friends yet. Her wardrobe began to look much like Emilie's, a series of pinafore-like shifts. Everyone assumed that her clothing was a deliberate co-ordination with the child's. Her term continued to go well and suddenly the ninth month had arrived. Her doctor told her that chances were so far very good. Albert prayed nonstop for the safety of his wife. Her happiness had infused her with a beauty and glow beyond any that he had seen before. This time had to be different. He was especially afraid that Cora would not be able to withstand another disappointment. His prayers were answered when Cora safely delivered a healthy baby boy. Now the cottage that he had built for them finally contained all of their dreams.

Emilie knew that something was happening. She could feel it. Tante Marie had come and some other woman had come during the day before. They didn't let her see Mommy Cora. When Daddy Albert finally took her into the room to see Mommy Cora, she had a baby lying beside her. Nobody needed a baby. She already had dolls, pretty dolls. They didn't understand why she was not more excited. She climbed down from his arms and went to play with her dolls. Maybe today she might see her brother when he peeked through the fence. Maybe today, she might let him know that she saw him.

Sally felt some emotion other than pain for the first time in all these months. She could hardly believe it when Albert came to tell her about the baby. In the midst of all this horror, something wonderful had happened. Her next realization was that Emilie would need to come home. Albert's mother, Marie, was there with them now. The proud grandmother assured Sally that Emilie was no trouble to her. Sally hadn't thought how much time had passed. How could she have been so blind? At least something good had come from this. She knew other stories about childless women having babies after caring for someone else's child.

It was time for her to handle her life and bring Emilie home. As bleak as it was, they would have to face life without Michael. Her fingers unconsciously stroked the silver bracelet on her wrist.

Carla Barone stopped by to see Sally. She was more subdued than before. The bubbly young woman was still warm, but her recent tragedy had dimmed the sparkle. Changes were apparent in her exterior self too. The gorgeous mane of coffee colored hair had been bobbed into an elegant coiffure just below her ears. Her explanation to Sally was that she needed to see a different person in the mirror every morning. A pervasive fear dominated Carla's thoughts after her husband's death, his family's possible retaliation. Nothing could change who they were and what their business was. Her relief came when her father advised her that the ailing, elder Barone was ashamed that his son had put his hands on his wife and child in such a cowardly manner. Real men, he assured her, did not do such things. He also sent money to 'help her through her time of trouble'. Shortly after this, word had reached her that Enrico's father had died and obtained deathbed vows that no one would harm her. Until Enrico was gone she had not realized how deeply his influences went. Recently she had discovered that even the family's meals were chosen to his tastes, never hers or the children's. Their lives were now a journey of discovery. She sold the large house and found a charming cottage not far from the flower shop. It was much more to her liking and provided a fresh backdrop for new lives. After selling her jewelry and the house, she was able to buy the shop with no problem. Carla excitedly told Sally that the majority owner had reduced the price of the shop by five percent. Of course this was no news to Sally, since she had been the majority owner. There was no question in her mind that she had done the right thing. Even with the price reduction, her profit had been sufficient to warrant the investment. Carla expressed such sadness when she heard about Michael's disappearance. Her impressions of Michael had been vivid and positive. Especially after her experience, she understood that his support of Sally's success had been priceless. After she left, Sally thought that the young woman had changed subtly. The sparkle was not gone, just deeper, more solid. Carla Barone had been through the fires that hardened her into a genuine gem of a human being.

17

In the indigent ward of New York Public Hospital, the man who had been labeled *James A. Doe* had begun to mend. His fractures had been compound and difficult to heal. A punctured lung had exacerbated the pneumonia for a prolonged period. The tracheotomy tube had remained for months. His body wasted away due to inactivity and the lack of solid food. The doctor who was just placed in charge of the case found this man's will to live fascinating. Generally, the indigent patients were not physically strong enough to survive such trauma and repeated setbacks. As the man had begun to mend, this normally overworked doctor had finally suspected that this particular patient was no wino or indigent. When his breathing tubes were removed, he started to try and talk. His voice was a hoarse croak, and the doctor explained that he needed to allow his throat some time to heal.

"Here, you'll need water. It might take a few days before your voice is useful." He gave the man a glass with a straw. As he drank, his eyes took in the sights of the ward. For the first time he could see the activities around him. A question was in his eyes, but he was unable to articulate.

At times, vocal chords were permanently damaged by the combination of a tracheotomy and the insertion of long term breathing tubes. This man might be such a casualty. Glancing at the chart, the doctor saw that his admit date had been almost a year and a half ago. Reviewing the chart carefully, he saw that this man should have been dead several times.

"James, I am Dr. Morrow. You are a very lucky man. We counted you out more than once." He wrote as he spoke.

"Ooaaaghh." The patient tried to speak, but only made a strange croaking sound. He shook his head, seeming upset.

The doctor tried to comfort the man. Patients who emerged from prolonged unconsciousness often experienced such distress. He would give him something to keep him calm for now. Sometimes it was best to keep such patients in a twilight sleep for a short time. Dr Morrow wrote the medication orders into the chart.

"I will see you tomorrow." He moved on to the next patient.

In his bed, the man examined his body. He knew that something was not correct. His body was not right and where was he?

As the days passed, his throat healed slowly. He attempted to make sounds daily. He found that many things were strange. It would have to be figured out a bit at a time. He recalled a floating sensation. The doctor kept calling him 'James'. He knew that this was not his name. It seemed that he was something of an oddity here in this place. Various nurses peeked in at him from time to time without saying anything. Only the doctor spoke to him. It took him several days after he gained consciousness to speak clearly. Dr. Morrow came to his bed. He looked at the chart carefully. After examining his patient, he gave him a drink of water.

"Is your voice working yet, James?"

The man took his time and spoke slowly.

"My name is Michael." His voice was still a bit rusty.

The doctor was startled. He glanced at the chart again. Nothing there indicated that he had been verbal. He looked at the man lying there in the bed. There was a visible spark in his eyes now.

"Well, hello Michael. I am Dr. Mor-..." He did not finish.

"Morrow, I remember. Where am I?" His manner was clipped and his speech was articulate.

The doctor stared at the man for a few moments, then looked for any note referring to amnesia. None had been made, but he had after all not been conscious. He wrote down the patient's statement and question. Then Michael saw the patch on Dr Morrow's jacket.

"New York? I am still in New York?"

The doctor began to be intrigued.

"Yes, you are in New York Public Hospital."

As a native New Yorker, Michael was aware of the stigma attached to the Public Hospital.

"Why am I here, in this place?" He asked impatiently.

He clearly had at least some command of his faculties, the doctor saw. He looked around him for a colleague, finding none. He plunged ahead.

"Okay, let's start at the beginning. What *is* your name?"

Michael looked at the man with annoyance. He looked about him for some clue that this was a mistake of some kind.

"I am Michael Tolliver. I live in New Orleans and where is my wife?"

The doctor knew that a different man was here in front of him.

"I am pleased to meet you Mr. Tolliver. You have been in this hospital for over one year as '*James Doe*'. You were found nearly naked and badly beaten in an alley in the Battery."

Michael tried to sit up in the bed. A searing flash of pain forced him to lie back down. The doctor put his hand on his shoulder.

"You must be careful. Lie back. You are now healing well, but there is still healing to do."

"I remember now. The taxi, I was waylaid in a taxi by some men. It made no sense." The memories came back haltingly.

"What were you doing here in New York, Michael Tolliver?"

Michael slowly explained that he had been traveling on business, but three thugs in the taxi had thwarted his trip to Chicago. His total manner changed as he suddenly blurted his request.

"My wife! I must speak to my wife! If I have been here all this time under this name, she must have no idea where I am! And my grandmother!" He was extremely anxious now.

"We will try to contact them if you will give me all of the information. In fact, I will do it myself."

The doctor quickly took down the information that Michael gave him, which included the name of a certain prominent judge. Dr. Morrow had never had a case quite like this before. This colored fellow seemed on the level, but there was always the chance that he was delusional. He would handle this himself, on his break. If the judge really knew this man, maybe the rest of his story was true. It did seem a bit unlikely, though.

Shortly after nine p.m., the insistent ring of the phone at the judge's residence startled Silas Quincy. His wife was already fast asleep. He sat reviewing the case that he was to hear in the court's morning session. Since any call so late generally signaled an emergency of some sort, he answered it promptly, but tentatively.

"Hello?"

"Yes, I am trying to reach the residence of Judge Silas Quincy. Is this he?

"Who is this?" He knew that the voice was a stranger.

"I am sorry, sir. I know that it is late. But I am David Morrow, a doctor on staff at New York Public Hospital. Does a Mrs. Carintha Tolliver live there?"

The man had his attention now. Obviously there must be something to the call. He put the briefs and case notes aside.

"Yes, doctor. What is it that I can do for you? Is it about a court order? But what does Carrie Tolliver have to do with it?"

"Are you by any chance acquainted with a man named Michael Tolliver? Is he Mrs. Tolliver's grandson?"

The judge focused his listening ear. Could he have said what he thought? After all this time, what news could he have? He braced himself for the worst.

"Dr. Morrow, did you say Michael Tolliver?"

"Yes, this patient says that is his name. He gave me your name as someone who would know him."

The judge had sadly presumed that Michael was dead. It had been more than a year.

"I believe that the man I know disappeared over a year ago. What does your patient look like?"

The doctor thought for a moment. He was not real sure except for the obvious.

"He's well over six feet tall. I would guess him to be thirty-five to forty. And he's a colored fellow."

"What happened to him?" The judge was afraid to get his, or Carrie's, hopes up. When the doctor gave the particulars of Michael's story and the medical aspects of the case, Judge Quincy advised that the man could possibly be Michael Tolliver. He asked that he speak to no one else about this until he could get there to the hospital. It did not make sense to get poor Carrie all wrought up over some imposter. Such a disappointment might well kill her. He rang his driver and put on his coat.

When Judge Silas Quincy saw the man who had been labeled as *James Doe* for over a year, he hesitated. The sleeping man was much thinner than Michael and had a full beard. Walking over to the bed, he noticed a few gray hairs that he had not seen on Michael.

"Hello."

When the man opened his eyes and smiled, he was Michael.

"Judge!" His voice was not as strong as normal.

The two men hugged affectionately as an amazed Dr. David Morrow watched from a distance. Neither had realized the depth of their feelings until now.

"My boy, you are alive!"

"Yes. But where is my grandmother? Has something happened?"

A fearful tone crept into his voice.

"No, No." Silas patted his shoulder, attempting to quiet his anxiety.

"When you disappeared, she did have a bad turn. But all is fine now. I simply wanted to be certain of your identity before I told her. In my opinion, she could not have survived such a disappointment."

When the visit was over, Michael knew as much of his family's news as Silas Quincy knew. He had hated to tell the younger man about the degree of his grandmother's illness. The good news was that she was almost back to normal. This news would surely make her even better. He made quick work of arranging to move Michael to another facility immediately. If he could have had a better quality of care, Silas felt that he would have mended more quickly. After a quick phone call, Michael was in the private care facility of a doctor friend by midnight. When Silas returned home in the wee hours of the morning, his wife almost woke up as he tried to give her the news. He could tell both of them in the morning.

The next morning Sally sat at her desk as usual. She had come in to the office a bit later today. It was the first week of the new schedule. Emilie had returned home. Sally found a new lady to care for the house, as well as to provide care for Emilie during the day. She had finally spoken to the boys about Michael after Cora's baby was born. It was difficult to explain that she had no answers, even after all this time. She spoke to them honestly about her feelings and how much she had hurt. Even harder for her was apologizing for her silence and for sending Emilie away. Cora had helped her while she was in such pain, she recounted. Her promise to her sons then was that she would bring the girl home soon, and she did. Their lives were going to return to something closer to normal, she also vowed. Antoine asked her if Michael could still be his daddy. She wondered what was in his mind, and told him that it was his choice since the adoption was completed. He said that Michael was the only father he had ever known, so he would keep his memories and his name. Bernard said nothing.

Antoine had been beside himself when the tiny girl walked into the music room. The metronome sat on the piano going tick, tick. A breeze wafted through the open windows. She wore one of the white pinafore dresses that Cora had crafted for her. Because he concentrated so hard when he practiced, at first he ignored the steps that he heard. It began to seep into his brain that it had not been Bernard or his Mother coming in. When he looked up to see the doll-like figure dressed all in white, he jumped from the piano stool and screamed. He took her up in his arms and turned her around and around. She sailed through the air like some giant, lacy kite. Then she began to laugh, starting as a giggle and growing into a full-throated chuckle.

Sally stood watching them until her face was covered in tears. This was the first time that she had allowed herself the luxury of joyful tears in a very long time. Bernard heard the ruckus and came running from the bedroom. The little girl sat atop the piano laughing, allowing her brothers to take turns amusing her. Now that the baby was with Mommy Cora, it was good to have her brothers back.

It was still strange for Emilie, who once again stood and stared at Sally as if asking a silent question. Sally began to wonder if she should try to give her some kind of an explanation. As she was leaving this morning the child had asked her if they could go to her "own house' today. Sally answered her by saying that this house was *her* house. Nothing in her facial expression indicated that the answer satisfied her. She simply waved goodbye to her mother and returned to eating her breakfast. Sally considered that perhaps she referred to Cora's house as hers now.

The judge's driver brought Carrie Tolliver to the bedside of her precious grandson immediately the next morning. As she had healed, Carrie became a mere shell of herself. Her emotional heart had been ripped out when she had received the phone call from Sally that day over a year ago. There was little surprise that her physical heart had failed, too. Her body had mended, as surely as her spirit had withered. It was a shock to see the delicacy of her frame, the shadowed cheekbones. God had taken her husband, her son and his wife and finally her grandson. She couldn't think of going down to live with Sally now, even though she was repeatedly asked. It would be too much of a reminder for both of them.

This morning, Silas Quincy hung the sun back in her sky. Until she saw him herself, Carrie was afraid to believe it. On the ride to the hospital, she wanted to pinch herself. Like Silas, she initially questioned the appearance of the thinner man. Seeing her, he broke into a Michael smile. Carrie felt the same way that she had on the day he had been born. A sparkle leapt into her eyes, a radiant glow into her cinnamon colored skin. He asked questions about his family. Carrie suggested that they try and call just as the phone was delivered to his room. They placed the call quickly.

Sally sat at her desk, deciding what her schedule would be today. She needed to determine her direction. Without Michael some of the business made no sense for her to continue to own it. She considered the four structures as the phone rang.

"Hello, *Café Petite Rouge*. May I help you?"

"Hello," his voice began to fail him. The tears came down his face unashamedly.

"Sally? Sally? Is that you?" His voice was tremulous, but familiar.

She couldn't answer at first. The male voice was too familiar. Could it be? Was this some prank?

"Who is this?" She asked in her most controlled business voice.

"Sally, it's me. Sally, I love you." Michael's voice was now strong and clear. How could he be calling after all this time? She wanted to hang up the phone. Just when she had begun to try and heal, the wound was reopened. This had to be some cruel joke.

"Who is this?" She asked, somewhat angrily.

"Michael, Sally it's me, Michael. Something happened to me."

Sensing that he had lost her emotionally, he began speaking faster.

"I am in a hospital. It's a long story. I have been unconscious and half dead, they say, for over one year. The doctors can tell you."

He handed the phone to the chief of staff who had walked into the room a few moments before. The doctor, a boyhood friend of Silas's, recounted the facts of the case for her. He gave her the vital information for the facility and then passed the phone to Carrie. Both of the women were in tears momentarily. After hanging up the phone, Sally stroked the silver strands of the bracelet on her wrist and cried until she had no tears left. The tight rein with which she had held her emotions was now unleashed. Between the children and Michael, her face had been awash in joy twice in such a short time.

Her first concern was for Michael. She needed to see him for herself! How badly was he injured? Would he need a nurse? Was he going to be okay soon? When could he come home? She stopped her mind from racing away with her. He was alive! That was all that mattered. Her very own Michael was alive!

When Michael had recounted the beating to Silas Quincy, the judge's mind had begun to make some conclusions. The entire occurrence definitely did not sound like a random incident. After Michael said that he might be able to identify the men, he put some of his influence to work. By the following evening, Chief of Detectives Tom Riley sat in the chair next to Michael. Riley was amazed at the detail with which this man remembered the attack after so much time. After hearing the whole story, a very similar case came to mind. On his next visit he brought a roster of faces for Michael to review. Two of the dozen he was able to identify. One of the two was Tony Barone. After Michael heard the man's surname, he asked the policeman if there was possibly a relationship between Tony and the New Orleans resident with that same surname. Since Enrico's prior history was no secret, the relationship was confirmed. Michael then recounted his wife's experience with Enrico. Riley advised him of Barone's death, but he figured out that enough time had existed for Barone to contact his brother and arrange the beating. Subsequent investigation revealed the phone company record of the call. Unquestionably, the police felt that the assailants had expected Michael to die. Few people survived such trauma and no attempt had been made to conceal their faces. Due to the very recent death of his father, Tony was now the head of the Barone crime family. Riley knew that if he could pin Tony with this felony assault charge personally, he would gain stars for his own cap while ridding the city of a menace. It would also not hurt to solve the crime and gain Judge Quincy's favor. After pulling in the accomplice that Michael had identified, he was able to coerce him to testify against Tony on Michael's assault, as well as to name the third man. With the continued cooperation of the accomplice, another felony murder with the same general *modus operandi* was tied to that trio. When the dust settled, Tony

Barone left town to serve multiple life sentences in Sing Sing Prison. The Barone crime family was immobilized.

Once she recovered from the astounding news that Michael was alive, Sally suddenly thought about all of the other people who loved her husband. Those people deserved to know the good news immediately. Hambone and Janette Williams were first on her list. Jonah took the last sip of his coffee and began preparing to leave for his office at *The Reserve*. Wondering who could be calling, he answered the telephone in the middle of the first ring.

"Hambone, he's alive!" Sally's voice was still filled with amazement..

"What? Who is … Sally? What are you saying?" Their friend found it hard to believe that this animated person could be Sally, or that she could be referring to Michael.

"Michael! I just spoke to him! He has been in a hospital, unidentified all this time! For all this time! He almost died! He was unconscious and unable to speak! Some men beat him. Hambone, they beat him unmercifully! Why would anyone want to harm him?"

Her elation had turned to confusion. Hambone listened, shaking his head. Of all the people he knew, Michael was the least likely to be in any fight because his sense of personal dignity usually eliminated such possibility. He couldn't figure out the why of the occurrence anymore than she. In the months to come, both would be aghast to discover the identity of the perpetrators.

Hanging up the phone, he said a quick prayer of thanks. No one knew how many times in the last year he had asked for God's ear on Michael's behalf. After letting his wife in on the new developments, he took off to *The Reserve* to spread the word. Within an hour, the word had reached the majority of the Tolliver business associates and their acquaintances. Hambone sat drinking a strong cup of coffee at his desk. Something nagged at him. He realized that there was one other person who would sincerely want to know that Michael was alive. He had to make the trip to St Bernard and Galvez Streets. It wouldn't be right not to include Jeff in the news.

The house sat back from the street. It actually had a small yard, unlike most of the others. Both the fence and gate were in good repair. Hambone noticed that the white paint was fresh as well. The last time he had dropped Jeff off, it hadn't looked like this. True that had been almost a year ago, but the change was remarkable. As he walked up to the porch, bright splashes of color winked at him from the garden. When he knocked at the door, a pleasantly smiling Jeff opened the door and welcomed him in. Unsure what to make of it, he stepped into a spotless and well coordinated room, not the seedy, drab bachelor digs of a few years ago. Jeff embraced him and offered a seat, as well as a glass of lemonade. Hambone felt as good as he could ever remember. Two good things happened today. Jeff looked as though he had actually put on a few pounds, finally. He was cleanly shaven with his hair freshly cut. Hambone couldn't help but smile. Glad that he had come, he joyfully began speaking.

"Jeff, man it's great to see you looking so prosperous. But I came over here to pass along some damn good news. Michael is alive! I know it's hard to believe after all this time."

Jeff's mouth fell open in disbelief. It'd been awhile since he had been around anyone in his old set. Michael's disappearance had hit him particularly hard since it had happened right on the heels of their conversation about Michael's blessings. Right away, Jeff had made a conscious effort to change himself, his life. Now, he held his head in disbelief. Jumping up, he shook his fists in a victorious gesture and thrust them to the sky.

"Oh, man! There is some right in this world!" He was truly joyous.

In the midst of this dance, a serene, smiling woman emerged from the hallway. She walked over to the already incredulous Hambone and stuck out her hand.

"Hi, I'm Kathryn. I already know who you are, Jonah. I apologize for eavesdropping, but what wonderful news!"

Hambone could not believe this development. Jeff had never in his forty years, had a stable relationship with a woman. Jeff saw the incredulous expression on his old friend's face. He put his arm about the beautiful woman's waist, and stood next to her.

"Jonah Williams, please meet Kathryn Arnaud. We were married six months ago. Life is good."

Hambone thought that he must look like a fish, because his mouth moved repeatedly with no sound coming out. Eventually he was able to speak.

"This is unbelievable. Congratulations! Why didn't you tell us? We all could have used some good news, especially back then."

"I guess that I was feeling guilty that I was so happy. You know it's been a steady gig at that spot uptown since just after Michael's disappearance. I met Kat there and it was love at first sight. Anyway, it was for me! My lady took some major convincing!" He laughed as he recounted. "Kat sings. She has some major pipes! I fell in love with her voice first."

"And I certainly fell for the sweetness of his saxophone before I was sold on his skinny behind." The voice was sweet and smoky even just speaking.

Kat Arnaud was a lovely woman whose vitality and earthiness gave her a special magnetism. Her curvy body was encased in silky ginger colored skin and her movements were fluid and graceful. Large doe eyes dominated her beautiful facial features. Standing next to her, Jeff seemed her perfect physical match. His golden angles were countered by her curves and softness. Hambone saw before him an obviously happy, very attractive couple. He clapped his hands.

"You have no idea how excited I am! I came over here believing that I was the one with the big news!"

"You did bring us the biggest news! What happened?"

Jonah gave the details as Sally had told them to him shortly before. He left after making plans for he and his wife to get together with the newly married couple soon.

It dawned on Sally that she had left out the most important people. The Sisters would just have to be angry with her for disturbing the classes today. She drove the short distance to *St Theo's*. The principal was not only tolerant of Sally's intrusion into the schedule, but Sister Angelique took a moment with her to offer a prayer for Michael's continued, complete and swift recovery. She had witnessed the positive changes in both boys after Sally's marriage. Both of them had become more confident and outgoing. Those boys were among her favorites and she took delight in pulling them from classes this morning.

Both boys were confused. It was unlike their mother to take them from school. Sally did not play when it came to school, that much was certain. Immediately, Antoine assumed that something had to be very, very wrong. The boy walked reluctantly with the small group. Why would Sister have his mother here? He and his brother were going with her for what reason? Nothing came to mind. He tried unsuccessfully to read something from Sally's face. Things got even stranger when Sister left them in her office alone. He began to be afraid.

Sally looked at her sons. Tentatively, she started out explaining the morning's events. The boys were as excited and disbelieving as she had been. By the time that she had told them all that she knew, the three of them were clinging together in tears and laughter. Since it was such a special occasion, Sister had agreed with Sally that it was probably best that the boys go home with her. Certainly neither of them would be able to concentrate their attention on schoolwork today.

Never had the drive to Orleans Street been more joyous. The boys giggled, jostled one another, made jokes and talked incessantly. It suddenly dawned upon Sally how glum their lives had become. At no time since Michael's disappearance had they been happy together like this. Only Emilie's homecoming made a dent in the canopy of gloom. She felt guilty. The pall that had settled down over her life when she lost Michael destroyed her personal awareness. She now knew that the boys had suffered and she prayed that she could make it up to all three of her children. But most of all, she needed to make it up to her husband. His suffering had been the most acute. Every time she made the effort even to contemplate what he had been through, she found herself in tears. In the back of her mind she knew that her fear had been that somehow Michael had stopped loving her and chosen not to return. Several times, she had looked at her rings and the "promise bracelet" and considered removing them. From time to time during his absence, the ugly doubts were refreshed by her pain and burned into the edges of her consciousness. Remembering these feelings now, Sally realized that she had been incredibly selfish during that time.

That night after the boys were in bed, she had the operator place a call to the hospital in New York. She was surprised to hear his voice answering the phone. Silas Quincy's influence made another special arrangement possible for Michael. His voice was normal now, its baritone timbre as warm and deep as usual.

"Michael Tolliver here."

"Hello Mr. Tolliver. How does it happen that you are answering the telephone?"

"Sweetheart, I am so glad that you did call me. I was lying there wondering what you were doing."

"Michael, I was missing you just as I have for the past year and a half. Only now, I at least have hope." Her voice broke. "I was sooo afraid that I would never see you again. Sometimes, I can still smell your fragrance and it causes a knot in the pit of my stomach."

He could hear the emotion in her voice and knew that her beautiful gray eyes were probably overflowing with tears, sparkling in that special silver color. Any thought of her pain tugged at his heartstrings.

"Darling, please don't cry. Sally, you know that only the devil himself could have kept me from you, from my family.

I wish that I were there to hold you."

"Michael, I am sorry. I didn't call to upset you. It's just that I am still so worried about you. Are you really going to be okay? Really?"

"Yes, darling. I sat up most of the day today. Tomorrow I will start physical therapy."

"Oh, this is such good news! I want to come to New York, Michael. I want to be with you, to help you any way that I can. I could pack and leave tomorrow evening. I need to see you."

His first thought was that he'd be glad to see her. Then, after a few moments, common sense settled in.

"Sweetheart, I need to see you too. What about the kids? Did you tell them?"

"Yes. The boys were really excited. Not even Christmas or Carnival has gotten that kind of reaction from either one of them. Michael, a few weeks ago we had a conversation about you. It was the first time that I had been able to talk to them about your disappearance. They let me know then that they love their dad."

Now it was his turn to shed the tears.

"Sally," he said after a few moments. "You know that means the world to me. What about the baby? Has she asked about me? Has she grown a lot? Daddy's little princess, God I miss her too."

Reluctantly, Sally proceeded to tell him about Emilie's stay with her cousin and the recent return. He heard in her voice more of the damaging effects of this whole tragedy. But he was happy to hear about Cora and Albert Rolande's fine baby boy. Something good had come from all this! He did, however feel that Emilie had been through enough. It was clear to him that they had to put the kids first. The decision was a hard one, but he had to remind himself that he was not the most important one.

"Sally, I want to see you so badly. Right now, I believe that we need to keep the kids settled. They have been through so much. I will be better soon and I will be home before we know it. Besides if I have you all to look forward to, I will work harder to get better. Darling, I need to come to you whole."

Sally felt hurt. She had thought through it all. Her father would come into town to stay. The boys and the new girl would be fine to pitch in for all of the chores. Why didn't he want her up there? She replied slowly.

"Whatever you think is best. I'd better say goodnight."

After she hung up, Michael lay awake wondering if he said some thing wrong. It was early morning before he finally closed his eyes.

For the next few days, Sally moved into a new fog. It was great to see the children together. She needed to continue putting one foot in front of the other, putting their lives back into the old rhythm. Carrie and Michael called to chat with the children a few days later. She didn't spend much time on the call herself. The boys were very excited, but Emilie didn't seem to grasp the principal of the telephone. She pushed the receiver away from her face and walked away. If it really was her own daddy in that funny thing, why didn't he come out and hug Emilie?

Confusion was also reigning in Sally's mind. Why didn't Michael want her to come? Was there something more that he wasn't telling her? He had been there so long. Maybe there was a nurse or someone that he had fallen in love with. She tried to maintain a positive face for the children especially. Friends around her noticed that she had become a bit more subdued, but chalked it up to the burden of duties she had borne for the last year and a half.

Carrie noticed it first. Sally just wasn't herself. In the two weeks, she had not placed a call to Michael, or to her. When they called, she made a few remarks to each of them and then always put the children on the phone. She didn't want to worry her grandson unnecessarily. But something told her that his happiness was absolutely at stake. Michael was working really hard on his recovery and was exhausted most of the time. The doctors could not believe the progress that he was making in such a short time. On his bedside table sat the beautiful portrait of Sally and the children. Carrie came in this evening and found him simply staring at it, smiling. It was one of the first things she had brought to him.

"They are a fine family, Michael," she remarked. "Seeing how happy it makes you, I am glad that I thought to bring it to share with you. Sally said that she was going to have a new one done. You remember that this is the photograph that you all sat for before your accident?"

"I remember. Actually, I was carrying a smaller version of it when I was attacked. Oh, Gran! You could not have been anymore correct. It is medicine to my soul to see them. I thank God for them all and I just can't wait to see them. I know that the kids have really grown."

Carrie saw his sincere enthusiasm and could not hold her curiosity. "Son, I need to know something. Why did Sally say that you didn't want her up here? She sounded so sad." Her eyes were concerned.

Michael turned and looked at his grandmother. His eyebrows were angled quizzically.

"What? What do you mean? "

"It's been worrying me. I noticed that she has hardly spoken to us when we call together. At first, I thought that the two of you maybe spoke at other times. Yesterday, I realized that you have been spending all day with the therapists and I hadn't had a good talk with her in a while. She was so down when I reached her. Michael, did something happen?"

"God no! I love Sally to no end," his voice trailed off.

"Think, Michael."

He sat there and suddenly remembered the conversation when he had told her that he thought it best that she not come up to New York. His hands flew up to his face.

"Oh, my God! Could she have misunderstood me? I was just worried about them all. The kids have been separated from one another, as well as from me. You know Emilie was with her cousin for most of the time that I was gone. I thought that they needed stability most of all right now. I wanted her here so badly, but I was trying to be adult, be a good father."

His voice was breaking. Carrie knew that he was almost in tears. It was difficult for her to see him suffering so.

"Son, I am going to go and get a cup of coffee. You call and talk to Sally. I'll be back later."

She leaned over and touched his cheek before departing the room. Michael went into the bathroom and washed his face. 'How could I have been so stupid,' he questioned himself. It was bad enough that she had been alone so long. In her mind she probably felt that he had rejected her. He only hoped that his mistake hadn't cost him her love. He sat down and picked up the receiver. A cheery operator efficiently filled his request and he heard the telephone ringing. On the third ring, Bernard picked up.

"Hello, may I help you?" His manner was serious and adult.

"Bernard. It's Dad. I want you to say hello to your brother and sister for me. It shouldn't be too long before I see you. I love you all, but tonight I really need to speak to your Mother. It's important."

Bernard heard the gravity in the tone of his voice.

"Dad, we love you too. I'll go get her."

Sally sat at the foot of her bed staring off into space. She had decided that she would turn in after saying hello to the children. Somehow, she just didn't have much energy today. When Bernard tapped at her door, she was barely aware. He tapped a second time.

"Mom!" He called out.

"Come on in. What is it?" She answered him listlessly.

"The telephone! Dad is on the telephone."

"Well, I am sure that he wants to speak to all of you. I didn't hear it ring."

"Mom, he wants to speak just to you."

Sally's heart leaped in fear. Maybe he was going to tell her the truth. Oh well, she thought. The truth had to come out.

"I will take it in here. Go hang up the other phone."

She moved around to the side of the bed and picked up the receiver.

"Hello. Michael? Hang it up, Bernard."

The boy replied, "Okay Mom. Bye, Dad."

Michael took a deep breath and plunged forward.

"Sally? Sally I miss you so!"

Her heart moved up from the pit of her stomach. He sounded as though he meant it.

"Michael, I wanted to come to you."

"Oh, I know and I wanted you here. I was just worried about us as a family. Please understand that. Carrie brought it to my attention that you seemed so down, so worried. Sally, please know that I love you with all my heart. I pray that you have not stopped loving me."

His plea was obviously sincere. She had begun to cry as he pored out his feelings. The doubts were now quieted. When she spoke, her spirit had been mended.

"I can come now, or not. It will be okay. When you told me not to come, I thought that maybe you had found someone else. It was just that you had been gone so long. Just as long as I know that you love me, I can wait for you."

"Don't ever doubt that! I have been working hard to come home, especially to you, whole. You would not believe how well I am doing. Please forgive me if I didn't explain correctly."

He could hear her sobs and his heart was shredded. Sally calmed down. Over the next few minutes as they spoke, they became one again. All the heaviness was lifted from both hearts. When Carrie returned to his room, Michael was smiling again. This time everything was totally right with his world.

18

The new house sat completed and empty. She always thought of it as Michael's house and Sally had not been able to face it for the last year. Now, it became real again. Though she didn't have a clue as to exactly *when* Michael would be able to come home, she knew that he <u>would</u> come home. Since Cora was now busy in the role of new mother, Helene Beauchamp stepped in to act as Sally's creative resource. Already familiar with the house because of Charles' work on it, she eagerly pulled together the elements necessary to make it uniquely reflect the Tolliver family's tastes and interests. Sally kept their work a secret from her children. She hoped to have the house ready as a gigantic surprise when Michael came back to New Orleans. The reports from the hospital were filled with glowing news of his progress. Simply moving him to the private facility afforded an increased level of medical attention under which Michael improved daily. Silas Quincy's influence continued to open doors. He told Sally that the care that Michael received in the public facility amounted to only slightly more than warehousing. His current medical team repeatedly advised that his survival was absolutely a miracle. If he had not possessed remarkable strength of body and spirit, under no circumstances would he be alive today. Since moving to the new hospital, he gained considerable weight and through intense physical therapy, was now walking comfortably again. Every indication was that he would recover fully.

A crew of workers was busy from dawn to dusk at the large corner house. Helene was a quick study and she had amassed an imaginative arsenal of decorative resources to meet the challenge. Very little work had been necessary on the upper floors so she set to work obtaining suitable furnishings, linen and décor. Sally wanted the entire residence to reflect a sense of tranquility. Her goal was to deflect the tragedy and chaos suffered by her family. Nothing in her home was going to mirror the stuffy Victorian brocades that were so prevalent when she was growing up. The airy lightness of tropical homes was what she sought to achieve. With Helene's artistic input the house became exactly what she desired. The rooms of glossy dark, wooden floors, high ceilings and pale walls were filled with ferns and palms. She found finely crafted furniture of rattan and pale oak. The only rooms to have darker colors were the new music rooms, where the mahogany shades of the instruments were blended with cordovan leathers and richly woven tapestries to create a Moroccan theme.

In Emilie's room, everything was white. From the white wicker furniture to the Battenburg lace coverlets, the little girl's room was a study in the pristine. Sally fell promptly in love with the myriad of white pinafore dresses that Cora made for her daughter. When she indicated that she wished to use similar fabrics in the toddler's new bedroom, Cora immediately jumped to the task. To further create a pleasing world for Emilie, Albert Rolande put his carpentry skills to use. Dismantling the gazebo that he built for Emilie at his home, he re-assembled it in a special garden at the new house. Albert and Cora believed that Sally was directly responsible for their remarkable good fortune. Both felt that caring for Emilie had been the catalyst for her successful pregnancy. Their son had been named Albert Emile Rolande in honor of that belief.

Sally could hardly wait until the little girl saw these delightful treasures. Since the child was so young, her mother was unsure how much to try and explain to her. The adjustment to coming home had been smooth enough. The boys took such pleasure in amusing her endlessly. She sat patiently in her small blue painted chair and allowed them to make her laugh. When Antoine played the piano, she dragged her little chair to that room where she sat quietly and listened patiently until he finished. Sally questioned whether she should try and explain that her daddy was going to come home. After all, the child might expect him to appear immediately and Sally couldn't bear to disappoint her.

Emilie saw that her real Daddy was not at this house. Things were different without her Daddy. Nobody in the world loved her quite like Antoine and her Daddy. She knew that. Sometimes Emilie didn't quite understand all the things that happened with big people, but she did know where she belonged and who loved her. Maybe her real Daddy was waiting for her at her own house. Then it would be okay. At least her Mommy didn't cry all the time anymore. Emilie had been glad to go to Mommy Cora before because her Mommy cried so much that she couldn't see Emilie. She didn't like it when people didn't see her. If they didn't see her, they couldn't love her. Some days Emilie sat in the little blue chair and just thought about these things.

Carrie Tolliver knew that her God lived. Michael was beginning to look like himself again. He was not the only one undergoing a metamorphosis. Suddenly Carrie's radiance had redeemed her beauty. The large deep set eyes were framed by a perfect curve of brow above the lovely cheekbones. Her shock of white hair looked healthy and vital. People who saw her these days never failed to remark on her mature beauty. She, meantime, was oblivious to all. Every waking moment she had was spent considering her blessings. This joy, that permeated her being, was visible on her countenance. After all seemed to be taken away from her, God had sent him back.

She spoke to Sally almost daily to give her the latest reports. When Carrie questioned the extraordinary expense, Silas Quincy told her that he and Carol had decided that they might as well spend the money on something worthwhile. He laughed when he informed her that since he and his wife had no children, it wasn't as though they needed to preserve an inheritance for progeny. In many ways he felt that his relationship with Michael was the closest he would ever come to having one with a son. His wife Carol, like he, was an only child so they had no close relatives whom they wished to endow. They had agreed to use all the resources necessary to see the Tollivers through this crisis. Some of his most pleasant memories involved observing Carrie's very bright grandson throughout the years. Carol often remarked that she would have been happy to have a son like Michael. It started with her admiration of the cute little boy having meals, or doing schoolwork when she spoke to Carrie about some household matter or another. His manners, his looks and then his intelligence won her over. Silas recalled that her chatter about the day's activities always included some anecdote about the little boy who lived downstairs. Initially, he was irritated, then appreciative that she had something harmless to occupy her. His wife began to lose the perennial sadness that had set in when she knew that her hope of having children was gone. Bit by bit she created a different kind of family for them that included Carrie and Michael. Silas remembered the diplomatically skillful way that she and Carrie had achieved the affectionate harmony of the household without his conscious awareness. The loss of Michael and Carrie's subsequent heart attack devastated both he and his wife. Now he was thankful that they could all return to normal.

Carrie remembered to take the new photograph to the hospital with her. When it arrived in the mail today, she had put it on the table near the door to her quarters. She couldn't wait for Michael to see the magnificent sepia portrait of Sally and the three children. It was hard to believe that the boys were such young men now. Of course Sally looked like some kind of motion picture star, but the real star of this picture was that precious little girl. Carrie could not believe that she was even real. The perfect little heart shaped face, those eyes and all that hair made her look like a storybook princess. That was it, Carrie decided, she looked like a little gingerbread storybook princess. Her great grandmother couldn't wait to kiss those cheeks.

Michael was dressed with a sweater and slacks under his robe and wore shoes instead of slippers today. Increasingly, he was up all day. After his therapy, he spent the rest of his time in the solarium, reading. There was so much for him to catch up on, both in the world and in his business. Reading of the NY papers told him that his investments were in spectacular shape. Today he was reviewing papers that Hambone forwarded at his request.

He is thankful that everything is in great shape in the businesses. With the repeal of Prohibition, the transition of *The Reserve* has been successful. New Orleans tourist trade has remained steady and the club's reputation has become solid on the national jazz scene. The topnotch entertainment lineup has secured the quality of audiences necessary. He is excited to see that the vocalist he had just begun to promote is selling records like hotcakes, or better yet, since it was New Orleans, seafood po'boys. It had been clear to him in that first session that she possessed the talent. Thankfully, Sally's leadership inspired genuine loyalty in the high caliber of people around her. In another situation, his absence could have been disastrous. He knew that she was an extraordinarily capable person, but the whole thing must have been hard on her. He would make it up to her if it took the rest of his life. Even though he has no real memory of the last year, he is sure that their love is what gave him the will to live. None of the doctors seemed to be able to provide any medical justification. Or, perhaps it was the combination of that love and his grandmother's constant prayer. She had repeatedly told him that she never gave up on him despite her misery. Her daily entreaty to God, she said, had been "Please bring him back." As though he had conjured up her sprightly figure, he looked up to see a glowing Carrie Tolliver coming through the solarium door.

"There he was", Carrie could not help but think of the differences in these last few weeks. He looked up as she approached him.

"Grandma! Good to see you!" He rose from his chair and kissed her on her cheek. Pulling one up for her use, he sat back down and put aside the papers he had been reading when she arrived.

"Son, I have something special for you today." Her smile was infectious. His first thought was that she was going to feed him again. He put his hand to his abdomen.

"Oh, Gran! I can't eat another thing this morning!" He was gaining his weight and strength partly because she constantly supplemented the hospital menu. Once the doctors had told her okay, she saw to it that he got every dish he had ever remotely enjoyed. Carried opened the box and drew out the picture.

"It's not your stomach I'm looking to feed this morning."

She thrust the picture at him smugly. It was a 12 x 18 studio portrait recently taken by one of the best photographers available in New Orleans. The sepia tones of the picture had been enhanced with oil tints making it exquisitely natural. His family stared back at him. His eyes fell first on Emilie. He began to cry. Too much of her young life had been stolen from him. She had been two and a half when he had boarded that train. It was almost her fourth birthday now. His beautiful baby girl gazed up at him. Her serious golden stare was much too old for such a tiny child. Soon he would make her laugh. He saw that Antoine still appeared to be almost the same size as Bernard. In fact, his shoulders were broader than those of his older brother. The longer curls had been cut from Antoine's hair. A young man looked into the camera pensively, exposing him as still the dreamer. Bernard wore spectacles, but his square jawed smile was handsome and strong. Soon it would be time to look at colleges for his future business tycoon. Sally had told him how the two boys had earned money in some hare brained scheme to help her after he disappeared. If they only knew what a savvy business mind their mother had. He looked carefully at Sally last, supposing it to be much like dessert. Seeing her face, he felt like he had been on a starvation diet. Her face was the sustenance for which his soul had hungered for such a long time. Vaguely, he remembered searching for something when he would momentarily emerge from his foggy state. He knew that it should have been in his pocket and he needed it. The family's first portrait had been in his pocket on the day that he was beaten and left for dead. As he wandered in and out of consciousness, the comfort of his family's images had been what he had sought. Most of all, the mental vision of Sally's face had sustained him. He put the portrait to his lips gently. Soon, he would see them. Soon. Carrie was thankful that she had been given the gift of sharing Michael's reaction to the faces of his family. Only the actual reunion could possibly be any better. She would definitely be present for that event.

Antoine discovered the half written melody in the piano bench months ago. Obviously, it had been around for a while. He looked at it several times and returned it to the storage place. It could only be a piece that Michael had been writing. But he knew that his dad had seldom touched the piano in the last year before the ill-fated trip. The melody picked itself out in his head time after time. Eventually he could not ignore the notes that kept intruding upon his consciousness. Retrieving the piece of paper, he picked out the melody on the piano. His fingers took on a life of their own. The chords gave birth to themselves mysteriously. Michael's half finished song was almost completed. Antoine knew that this would be the most personal gift he could give his father upon his return. All of his spare time was devoted to this task.

Bernard felt good about the last few months. It was good to have Emilie back with them. She was such a funny kid. Antoine had taken her absence the hardest.

That was the way it was supposed to be. He was still a kid even if he was bigger now. It was weird the way they got things all mixed up. His mom had laughed at them when they had given her the forty-two dollars. Promptly the three of them went to Canal Street and that money was put into savings accounts for them. She said that she was proud that they wanted to help, but money was the last thing that she needed. Bernard thought he had never heard anyone say that before. He had learned a lot lately. A long time ago when they found out that she owned the restaurant, he was real impressed with his mom. Working with her that short time had been interesting enough. Now though, he knew that he could learn a lot from her, from Michael too. He was so glad that Michael would be home. It was so hard to see Mom hurting that way. Maybe her thought had been that Michael left because he wanted to. Bernard never once thought that. Anybody who saw them together must know how he felt about her. One thing Bernard was sure of was that Michael loved all of them. It felt right calling him Dad.

Surrounded by lesser buildings, the Hotel St John was an impressive structure. The four years that it had taken to remodel and refurbish the building were well spent. Celebrities and local luminaries wandered through the building, chatting, sampling the food and surveying the rooms. Snatches of conversation could be overheard indicating that they were in universal agreement that the Tollivers had done something really astounding for the city. Such an undertaking had been phenomenal in these economically challenged times. Hotel St John provided a welcome boost to the area skyline, as well as to its economy and the souls of the people.

Sally had delayed the grand opening for as long as she could. Matthew Dickson had everything in perfect operating order. The staff was hired and in place. It just couldn't wait any longer. Today was an unbridled success. It was too bad that Michael hadn't been able to make it home in time. However, he would be amazed to see how it had turned out when he did finally arrive.

In the Piano Bar, Kat Arnaud sang with Jeff's new trio backing her. Sally liked Kat and although she knew little about music, loved her sound. She was sure that Hambone was correct when he said that Michael would make her a big star. Most of all she was happy to see the changes in Jeff. Kat's success didn't seem to be the least bit of a problem for him. Instead he was her most ardent supporter. In fact, his performances seemed to be inspired by her. None of the old resentment seemed to be left in Jeff. Sally knew Michael had been very close to him in the past and had become concerned about the path his life had taken. This would be one more positive development to assure that his homecoming would be just right.

19

Crowds of people walked about the train depot. Even here it was totally different from the frenetic pace of the New York station. People were obviously on the way to destinations, but they proceeded in a civil manner. Suitcases in hand, they sauntered elegantly toward the proper embarkation points. The track signs swayed in the afternoon breeze. Metal behemoths sat panting in wait to serve. Smoke and steam drifted across the tracks. The announcer drawled out the names of cities as travelers moved toward the platforms in pursuit of a multitude of dreams.

Sally stood anxiously waiting. This was the right track number and time. She glanced down at the yellow rectangle of paper in her hand, creased and folded repeatedly. When the telegram came, her heart had thumped so wildly that she thought it would jump from her chest. The time had finally come. Silas Quincy wired her of the arrival time for Carrie and Michael just for good measure. They had given her the information by telephone, but the yellow paper made it more real. The day had come.

Smoothing her dress, she knew that it was a shallow concern, but it was important that he was pleased with what she wore. The cream jersey dress was tailored to perfectly skim the curves of her body. Rucching accented the seams of the bodice and sleeves. On her head she wore one of the new turbans fashioned of the same fabric. She had let her hair grow out again. Looking nervously into the mirror, she wondered if he would notice her freshly auburn tresses. Since Annie now operated a beauty salon nearby, Sally made it a point to patronize her establishment. It had been her idea to enhance the color with henna and Sally was pleased with the results. Michael had once said that he would love to have seen her as a redhead. Maybe she worried too much about her appearance, she thought as she powdered her nose one last time. Tucking the gold compact into her handbag, she could see the behemoth of a locomotive chugging laboriously into the platform. It would be a while before they got off the train she was sure. They said that Michael had gotten so much better, but he had been through so much. It certainly couldn't help that the train ride was so long. She would try to give him plenty of time to recuperate. The last thing she wanted to do was rush him. Shifting from one foot to the other, she watched as the uniformed Conductor swung himself down from the train.

Inside her bosom, the thump, thump of Sally Tolliver's heart seemed to fill the entire space of her being. Every person nearby must be able to hear and even feel the vibration. She looked about her, trying to see a reaction on someone's face, but no one else seemed to be aware of her personal maelstrom. Clutching her arms tightly about her body, Sally wondered if she were losing her mind. Time seemed to slow to a crawl. The conductor moved as if underwater, while her ears received sound through some filter stringing out the noise from overhead speakers into a necklace of syllables. Her body longed to be near enough to feel his presence. Her hands needed to touch him, to feel the texture of his skin, his hair. These tactile memories of him, her Michael, caused her body to shiver. What she could swear were vivid whiffs of his actual scent shocked her into consciousness, returned her to real time. It was an eternity. Ahead of her the conductor finally completed the motion of placing the step onto the ground. Before it settled, Michael came leaping off of the train startling the Conductor. He grabbed her up into the strong circle of his arms.

"Sally, Sally, Sally!" He repeated her name as though to assure himself that she was really there. Her eyes were fixed on his wonderful face. It was truly his face, she told herself as she traced the strong chin. Her fingers wandered up to the sliver of silvered strands at his temple. She recalled that his ears were especially sensitive to her touch when they made love. Touching him, every fiber of her being was thankful. Even though his frame carried a few less pounds, her husband looked none the worse for wear. That was it. He looked his same handsome self with just a fine streaking of white at one temple.

"You are here, Michael. You are finally here! You have no idea how much I missed you!"

He took her face in his hands.

"Yes, I do know." His lips glanced hers sweetly, then deeply while the depth of their hunger teased them both. No other words were necessary. They stood quietly clinging together as the crowd graciously split to go around them. Carrie came up at that moment with a smiling Redcap trailing behind with the cart full of bags. They eventually let go of one another, so that Sally could greet Carrie appropriately. Sally held Michael's grandmother at arm's length and remarked on how great she looked. Indeed, Carrie's traveling ensemble was a beautifully tailored suit of violet trimmed with black that flattered her slim figure to no end. A black hat crowned the halo of stark white hair charmingly. She smiled broadly, but shooed away Sally's enthusiastic compliments. The older woman felt herself to be the happiest member of the trio.

Sally hadn't told the children that this was the day. When she pulled her car up to the front of the house, Emilie stood on her little blue chair looking out of the window. Her heart shaped face rested sideways on her hands. She recognized her mother's car. Knowing that Sally didn't usually come home at this time of day, her interest was raised. She saw Sally, then a lady with a nice face and beautiful white hair come from the car. She climbed down and went to stand beside the door. Mommy always saw her now. That made Emilie very happy. Emilie was glad for Mommy to come home. But when the door opened, it wasn't just Mommy. Looking up she saw the smiling face of her own Daddy filling the space in the doorway. Finally, her Daddy had come home. She put her arms up happily. He picked her up and hugged her tight. Emilie had dreamed about this for a long time. Her real Daddy had come home!

Michael hugged his daughter tightly, while trying to grasp how anyone human could love another so much. Loving one's child took on a whole different dimension than loving a mate, he thought. That child is the best of oneself, the sum of your dreams, hopes and aspirations. This precious bit of humanity that he held in his arms was the most important part of his legacy. As he held her out to just look at her, Michael was convinced that she was absolutely the most beautiful child that had ever existed on earth. Emilie heard his thought in her heart and gave him the biggest smile that she could.

At exactly that second, the front door opened and Bernard came bounding in first, followed by his brother and grandfather, Rene. Acting totally unlike himself, he threw his arms first around Carrie, then Michael. Making room for his brother, he buried his face on Michael's shoulder and sobbed.

"Dad! Dad!" He repeated. "I love you!"

Handing Emilie off to Sally, Michael surrounded both of his sons in his embrace. Antoine said nothing. Like his brother, he buried his face against a shoulder.

Sally stood watching her husband and sons while Rene Arceneaux moved next to his daughter. The depth of her feelings was apparent. How wonderful to have all the members of her family together again.

Emilie moved to Carrie's arms when she held them out and beckoned. Emilie always knew when people cared about her. This was a really good time because the room was filled with people who cared about Emilie and Emilie loved them back. This lady was someone special to her, Emilie could tell, so she hugged her neck as hard as possible. Carrie, rejoicing in the love she was sharing, recalled the years that she and Michael had been such a small family. Her heart recognized that this was so much better. She tightly held onto the precious little girl.

Rene Arceneaux moved next to her smiling warmly and touched her arm. During the last two years, they had exchanged pleasant letters and the occasional phone call. A close relationship had developed and he thought that he would soon have to sit down with Michael and be the one to explain his intentions this time. He drank in the loveliness that radiated from Carrie. The two of them shared a smile, glad that this time she would remain here in the Crescent City.

A grand meal had been laid out. The new girl of help was Annie's youngest sister and she had easily stepped into the household. Sally had actually done some of the cooking herself and left instructions for the rest. Her thought was that this would be their first family dinner in two years. With her father and Carrie, completing the circle, Sally couldn't help but wish that they could have done this in the new house, but there would be many more dinners to have there and she wanted to present it as a surprise later. The meal was a joyful occasion, filled with lots of love, laughter and catching up. Since it was Friday, the fare was the traditional seafood dinner with Gumbo added since the day was special. A half dozen Pecan pies completed the marvelous fare. After the family had stuffed and gorged, Sally sprang her surprise. Everyone was to get in the cars. Her father drove his sedan with Carrie tucked next to him and the boys in the rear seat. Sally drove Michael with Emilie installed in the back seat of Sally's new white roadster as though it was her throne. Michael now noticed that the new car coordinated with Sally's wardrobe. Few people had the flair that his Sally did, he thought as he enjoyed simply being with her. When they arrived at the house, Michael was somewhat surprised. His wife had said nothing about the residence he had purchased, so he concluded that she had possibly sold it. Happily, he stepped out into the driveway. A garage was one of the amenities that had been created at the rear of the former basement area. He removed his daughter from the back seat and took her hand. The boys assumed that they were going to visit some friends of their parents. It looked like a very grand house. Sally's dad and Carrie brought up the rear. They stepped up to the door and Sally handed her husband the key. Michael opened the door and entered a totally furnished home. The first thing that the group saw in the foyer was a large portrait of the children painted by a friend of Helene's. Just as lifelike as the photograph had been, it was breathtaking in this setting. A chandelier hung from the center of the domed room that was appointed with leafy greenery. An exotic table sat under the painting as the perfect accent. Realization that this was the family's new home was greeted with a huge exclamation from the boys. Emilie took off running through the house with the most territorial of attitudes. Immediately upon entering, she began an exploration of the house. The family traipsed from room to room, marveling at each and every detail. Emilie discovered her room and came to get Carrie to share her new kingdom. She had quickly sensed that because Grandma Carrie loved Emilie very much, she could be her new best friend. When the group reached the music room, both Michael and Antoine saw that Sally had already gotten the piano moved into its new space. For Michael, it was like unexpectedly seeing an old friend. He sat down and picked out a melody. His fingers had lost just a bit of their flexibility, but Sally could remember. A shudder went through her body as her mind flashed back to the first night that they were together and he played for her. When Michael got up, Antoine sat down in front of the keys. He began to play. Neither Carrie, nor his grandfather had heard Antoine play before. Both of them sat in utter amazement, exchanging proud and affectionate glances. He gave a performance that Dr. Fein would have expected. His fingers danced across the keys with magical agility. Only Michael was not surprised because the boy played exactly as well as his father had known that he would. When he finished, the group sat in stunned silence. He looked around him, wondering what they were thinking. Michael started the applause first. He stood and clapped enthusiastically. Tears were in his eyes. His thought was that he had become a simpering idiot. All day he had been crying about every single occurrence. In the back of his mind, he did not care who knew. Antoine stood up for a second to remove a piece of paper from the bench.

"Dad, you might remember this." He said.

As the melody came to life, Michael recognized the last piece of music that he had started writing. His original intent was to create a piece for Sally. As the boy kept playing, Michael realized that his son had completed the work in an extraordinarily capable manner. When the music stopped, Michael told him how proud he was of his work. Carrie knew that the music was unfamiliar to her, but she had enjoyed it a great deal.

"What was the name of that nice song, son? I don't believe that I've heard it before."

She couldn't believe how well the boy played. It reminded her of the pride she had felt when Michael once performed as a young boy. Before Antoine could answer her, Emilie walked over to her great grandmother and took her hand. In a very grownup manner, she proceeded to explain.

"This is Emilie's Song. This is Emilie's own house and that was Emilie's song." She made her pronouncement then turned and walked over to her Daddy.

It then dawned on Sally that the child had mentioned her 'own house' once before when she asked where her 'real daddy' was. As Sally turned to remark about this, Emilie tugged at her father's pant leg. She looked up at him.

"You said it. Didn't you say it, Daddy?" Her little voice rang out.

"Say what, baby girl?" As he reached down and hoisted her up into his arms, he saw that her legs were just about too long to do this anymore.

"Daddy, remember before? You said this was Emilie's *own house*!" She was emphatic in her declaration. Michael then recalled that he actually had brought a barely two-year-old Emilie here with him after he had received the deed to the house. That she remembered was astounding!

"Yes, daddy did say that. Darling, daddy did truly say that."

Emilie spoke to the group from her lofty perch.

"See! I told you. It's Emilie's house and it's Emilie's song, too."

The entire group burst into laughter. No one dared argue with her, they were simply glad to be a part of Emilie's kingdom.

The End

About the Author

A poet and novelist, she is totally enamored of the nuances of language, both spoken and written. Repatriated to the Third Coast several years ago, this Texas native finds constant inspiration in the fascinating people and the beautiful landscapes of Texas and the South.

Lightning Source UK Ltd.
Milton Keynes UK
UKOW02f0017230416

272781UK00001B/7/P

9 781438 903323